MOTHER

OTHER BOOKS FROM VISION FORUM

MOTHER

A STORY

BY
KATHLEEN NORRIS

Restored and Revised Edition

THE VISION FORUM, INC.

4719 BLANCO RD.
SAN ANTONIO, TEXAS 78212

"Where there is no vision, the people perish."

THE VISION FORUM, INC.
4719 BLANCO RD.
SAN ANTONIO, TEXAS 78212

1-800-440-0022
www.visionforum.com

Dedicated to
Beall, Cecelia, and Marilyn

Three mothers who made an investment in
their children which will last for eternity.

FOREWORD

I have a wonderful mother. Her hospitality is famous, her home is a haven, and her company is delightful. Her many talents include dressmaking, upholstery, painting, gardening, teaching, organizing, and architectural design (she designed our family home!). And everything she does, she does at home, demonstrating what a full and rich sphere is a woman's true habitation. My mother is an inspiration to me.

But I did not always appreciate my mother as I do now. In fact, there was a time when I looked at my mother's work with disdain and wondered how she could find any enjoyment in baking bread, cleaning house, and taking care of my younger siblings. I was certainly not going to be relegated to such "drudgery." I was going to get out into the world and make my own way.

How did this change in attitude come about? I adored my mother all through childhood. I copied her and hoped to be like her when I was a teenager. I wanted to have all that she had: the loving husband (my wonderful father), the beautiful, peaceful home, the contented family life, and the joys of hard work. That changed after four years away from home in college. When I confided my ideals to my new friends at school, they either humored me (as they would a dreamer), or they laughed outright. All claimed I had been born in the wrong century, and that if I wanted to find a husband who would let me stay at home all day, I'd have to get into a time machine.

At first, I held on to my high ideals. After all, I had seen first-hand that they were realistic and beautiful through the example of my parents. But four years of college ground away mercilessly at my core beliefs, leaving them broken and embittering me. By the time I got out into the "real" world, I found that contentment eluded me. I had bought the lie that "woman's work" is antiquated, something to be avoided at all costs. I built a tough shell around my heart and scoffed at the ideals I had once held dear.

But God was not fooled. Over the next year and a half, He brought wonderful friends into my life who began to chip away at the shell. They did this with their love, with their letters, with their questions, with their examples. I resisted at first, thinking they were like others I had known—false friends who were only preaching at me. But God's grace is irresistible, and my shell began to crack.

One day, while browsing at a local book fair, a lovely dust jacket caught my eye. I've always enjoyed old books, so I picked this one up. The cover showed a young woman standing with her arms around her seated mother. The two were looking into each other's eyes. Behind them, the family sat around the dining table. The name of the book was *Mother*. It was only two dollars, and it looked interesting, so I added it to my pile.

That night, I opened the book, intending to read a chapter or two before bed. An hour passed before I realized how far I had read. I could not put the book down and finished it shortly before midnight. As I turned the last page, tears filled my eyes. I knelt by my bed and asked God to forgive me for my bitterness and my unwillingness to trust and obey Him. In the few hours it took to read the book, God melted away the last of my resistance. I felt like a new woman.

Mother is not a great work of literature, like something by Shakespeare or Austen or Dickens. It is not a work of high art or lofty prose. It is the simple story of one young woman's journey from discontentment to understanding and, finally, to joy. God used this book as a tool to show me how my own embittered thinking had poisoned me to what is really beautiful and worthwhile in life: service. "If anyone desires to be first, he shall be last of all and servant of all" (Mark 9:35). What an overlooked message in our self-centered times!

There is no shame in godly womanhood. There is no inferiority in being a wife, a mother, a daughter, or a servant. To call the Proverbs 31 woman "restricted" or "liberated" is to miss the point. She is the glorious queen of her realm. She rejoices in her place and handles her tasks with great ability—even with laughter! This is the message of *Mother*.

I've hunted through countless antique bookstores, searching for copies of this wonderful little book for friends and relatives. I know I've given away at least twenty books. Unfortunately, as the years passed and new editions of the book were printed, the heart of *Mother* was edited completely out of it by later publishers, and its truths were either covered over or lost completely. The book you now hold is a completely restored and revised edition, clearly proclaiming the message Kathleen Norris intended which caused millions of Americans to hail *Mother* as the "pro-life novel of the century."

What a joy to have *Mother* restored at last! I hope you enjoy this story and take time to meditate on the delights of servant-hood, selflessness, and godliness with contentment, which is great gain.

Jennie Chancey
At Home
Rileyville, Virginia
June 18, 2000

CHAPTER I

"Well, we couldn't have much worse weather than this for the last week of school, could we?" Margaret Paget said in discouragement. She stood at one of the school windows, her hands thrust deep in her coat pockets for warmth, her eyes following the whirling course of the storm that howled outside. The day had commenced with snow, but now, at twelve o'clock, the rain was falling in sheets, and the barren schoolhouse yard and the playshed roof ran muddy streams of water.

Margaret had taught in this schoolroom for nearly four years now, ever since her seventeenth birthday, and she knew every feature of the big, bare room by heart, and every detail of the length of village street that the high, uncurtained windows commanded. She had stood at this window in all weathers: when locust and lilac made even ugly little Weston enchanting, and all the windows were open to floods of sweet spring air; when the dry heat of autumn burned over the world; when the common little houses and barns and the bare trees lay dazzling and transfigured under the first snowfall, and the wood crackled in the schoolroom stove; and when, as today, midwinter rains swept drearily past the windows, and the children must have the lights lit for their writing lesson. She was tired of it all, with an utter and hopeless weariness. Tired of the bells, of the whispering, of the shuffling feet, of the books that smelled of pencil dust and ink and little dusty fingers; tired of the blackboards, cleaned in great irregular scallops by small and zealous arms; of the clear-ticking big clock; of little girls who sulked, and little girls who cried after hours in the hall because they had lost their lunch baskets or their overshoes, and little girls who had colds in their heads, and no hand-kerchiefs. Looking out into the gray day and the rain, Margaret said to herself that she was sick of it all!

There were no little girls in the school-room now. They were for the most part downstairs in the big playroom, discussing cold lunches, and planning, presumably, the joys of the closely approaching holi-days. One or two windows had been partially opened to air the room in their absence, and Margaret's only companion was another teacher, Emily Porter, a cheer-ful little widow, whose plain, rosy face was in marked contrast to the younger woman's unusual beauty.

Mrs. Porter loved Margaret and admired her very much, but she herself loved teach-ing. She had had a hard fight to secure this position a few years ago; it meant comfort to her and her children, and it seemed to her a miracle of God's working, after her years of struggle and worry. She could not understand why Margaret wanted anything better; what better thing indeed could life hold? Sometimes, looking admiringly at her associate's crown of tawny braids, at the dark eyes and the exquisite lines of mouth and forehead, Mrs. Porter would find herself sympathetic with the girl's vague discontent and longings, to the extent of wishing that some larger social circle than that of Weston might have a chance to appreciate Margaret Paget's beauty. But, after all, sensible little Mrs. Porter would say to herself, Weston was a "nice" town, only four hours from New York, absolutely up-to-date; and Weston's best people were all "nice," and the Paget girls were very popular, and "went everywhere"—young people were just discontented and exacting, that was all!

She came to Margaret's side now,

buttoned snugly into her own storm coat, and they looked out at the rain together. Nothing alive was in sight. The bare trees tossed in the wind, and a garden gate halfway down the row of little shabby cottages banged and banged.

"Shame—this is the worst yet!" Mrs. Porter said. "You aren't going home to lunch in all this, Margaret?"

"Oh, I don't know," Margaret said despondently. "I'm so dead that I'd make a cup of tea here if I didn't think Mother would worry and send Julie over with lunch."

"I brought some bread and butter—but not much. I hoped it would hold up. I hate to leave Tom and Sister alone all day," Mrs. Porter said dubiously. "There's tea and some of those bouillon cubes and some crackers left. But you're so tired, I don't know but what you ought to have a hearty lunch."

"Oh, I'm not hungry." Margaret dropped into a desk, put her elbows on it, pushed her hair off her forehead. The other woman saw a tear slip by the lowered lashes.

"You're exhausted, aren't you, Margaret?" she asked suddenly.

The little tenderness was too much. Margaret's lip shook. "Dead!" she said unsteadily. Presently she added, with an effort at cheerfulness, "I'm just cross, I guess, Emily; don't mind me! I'm tired out with examinations, and"—her eyes filled again—"and I'm sick of wet, cold weather and rain and snow," she added childishly. "Our house is full of muddy boots and wet clothes! Other people go places and do pleasant things," said Margaret, her breath rising and falling stormily, "but nothing ever happens to us except broken arms and bills and boilers bursting and chicken-pox! It's drudge, drudge, drudge from morning until night!"

With a sudden little gesture of abandonment she found a handkerchief in her belt and pressed it, still folded, against her eyes. Mrs. Porter watched her solicitously but silently. Outside the schoolroom windows the wind battered furiously, and rain slapped steadily against the panes.

"Well!" the girl said resolutely and suddenly. And after a moment she added frankly, "I think the real trouble today, Emily, is that we just heard of Betty Forsythe's engagement—she was my brother's favorite, you know; he has admired her ever since she got into High School, and of course Bruce is going to feel awfully bad."

"Betty engaged? To whom?" Mrs. Porter was interested.

"To that man—boy, rather; he's only twenty-one—who's been visiting the Redmans," Margaret said. "She's only known him two weeks."

"Gracious! And she's only eighteen—"

"Not quite eighteen. She and my sister, Julie, were in my first class four years ago; they're the same age," Margaret said. "She came fluttering over to tell us last night, wearing a diamond the size of a marble! Of course"—Margaret was loyal—"I don't think there's a jealous bone in Julie's body; still, it's pretty hard! Here's Julie plugging away through the Normal School, so that she can teach all the rest of her life, and Betty's been to California and to Europe, and now she's going to marry a rich New York man. Betty's the only child, you know, so, of course, she has everything. It seems so unfair, for Mr. Forsythe's salary is exactly what Dad's is; yet they can travel, keep two maids and entertain all the time! And as for family, why, Mother's family is one of the finest in the country, and Dad's had two uncles who were judges—and what were the Forsythes! However"— Margaret dried her eyes and put away her handkerchief—"however, it's for Bruce I mind most!"

"Bruce is only three years older than you are, twenty-three or four," Mrs. Porter smiled.

"Yes, but he's not the kind that forgets!"

Margaret's flush was a little resentful. "Oh, of course, you can laugh, Emily. I know that there are plenty of people who don't mind dragging along day after day, working and eating and sleeping—but I'm not that kind!" she went on moodily. "I used to hope that things would be different; it makes me sick to think how brave I was; but now here's Ju coming along and Ted growing up, and Bruce's favorite girl throwing his friendship over—it's all wrong! I look at the Cutter girls, nearly fifty, and running the post office for thirty years, and Mary Page in the Library, and the Norberrys painting pillows—and I could scream!"

"Things will take a turn for the better, Margaret," said the other woman, soothingly, "and as time goes on you'll find yourself getting more and more pleasure out of your work, as I do. Why, I've never been so securely happy in my life as I am now. You'll feel differently some day."

"Maybe," Margaret assented unenthusiastically. There was a pause. Perhaps the girl was thinking that to teach school, live in a plain little cottage on the unfashionable Bridge Road, take two roomers, and cook and sew and plan for Tom and little Emily, as Mrs. Porter did, was not quite an ideal existence.

"You're an angel, anyway, Emily," said she affectionately, a little shamefacedly. "Don't mind my growling. I don't do it very often. But I look about at other people, and then realize how my mother has slaved for twenty years and how my father has been tied down, and I've come to the conclusion that while there may have been a time when a woman could keep a house, tend a garden, sew and spin and raise twelve children, things are different now; life is more complicated. You owe your husband something; you owe yourself something. I want to get on, to study and travel, to be a companion to my husband. I don't want to be a mere upper servant!"

"No, of course not," assented Mrs. Porter, vaguely, with a troubled frown wrinkling her brow.

"Well, if we are going to stay here, I'll light the stove," Margaret said after a pause. "B-r-r-r! This room gets cold with the windows open! I wonder why Kelly doesn't bring us more wood?"

"I guess—I'll stay." Mrs. Porter said uncertainly, following her to the big book closet off the schoolroom, where a little gas stove and a small china closet occupied one wide shelf. The water for the tea and bouillon was put over the flame in a tiny enameled saucepan; they set forth on a fringed napkin crackers and sugar and spoons.

At this point a small girl of eleven with a brilliant, tawny head, a wide mouth and a toothless smile, opened the door cautiously and said, blinking rapidly with excitement, "Mark, Mother theth pleath may thee come in?"

This was Rebecca, one of Margaret's five

younger brothers and sisters and a pupil of the school herself. Margaret smiled at the eager little face.

"Hello, darling! Is Mother here? Certainly she can! I believe—" she said, turning suddenly radiant, to Mrs. Porter—"I'll just bet you she's brought us some lunch!"

"Thee brought uth our luncheth—eggth and thpith caketh and everything!" exulted Rebecca, vanishing, and a moment later Mrs. Paget appeared.

She was a tall woman, slender but large of build and showing, under a shabby raincoat and well pinned-up skirt, the gracious and generous lines of a figure that is rarely seen except in old daguerreotypes, or the ideal of some artist two generations ago. The storm today had blown an unusual color into her cheeks. Her bright, deep eyes were like Margaret's, but the hair that had once shown an equally golden lustre was now touched with gray. She came in smiling and a little breathless.

"Mother, you didn't come out in all this rain just to bring us our lunches!" Margaret protested, kissing the cold, fresh face.

"Well, look at the lunch you silly girls were going to eat!" Mrs. Paget protested in turn, in a voice rich with amusement. "I love to walk in the rain, Mark, as I used to love it when I was a girl. Tom and Sister are at our house, Mrs. Porter, playing with Duncan and Baby. I'll keep them until after school, then I'll send them over to walk home with you."

"Oh, you are an angel!" said the younger mother, gratefully. And "You are an angel, Mother!" Margaret echoed, as Mrs. Paget opened a parcel and took from it a large jar of hot, rich soup, a little blue bowl of stuffed eggs, half a fragrant whole-wheat loaf in a white napkin, a little glass full of sweet butter, and some of the spice cakes to which Rebecca had already enthusiastically alluded.

"There!" said she, pleased with their

delight, "now take your time; you've got three-quarters of an hour. Julie devilled the eggs, and the sweet-butter man happened to come along just as I was starting."

"Delicious! You've saved our lives," Margaret said, busy with cups and spoons. "You'll stay, Mother?" she broke off suddenly, as Mrs. Paget tied up the empty parcel.

"I can't dear. I must go back to the children," her mother said cheerfully. No coaxing proving of any avail, Margaret went with her to the top of the hall stairs.

"What's my girl worrying about?" Mrs. Paget asked, with a keen glance at Margaret's face.

"Oh, nothing!" Margaret used both hands to button the top button of her mother's coat. "I was hungry and cold, and I didn't want to walk home in the rain!" she confessed, raising her eyes to the eyes so near her own. "Well, go back to your lunch," Mrs. Paget urged, after a brief pause, not quite satisfied with the explanation.

Margaret kissed her again, watched her descend the stairs, and leaning over the banister called down to her softly,

"Don't worry about me, Mother!"

"No—no—no!" her mother called back brightly. Indeed, Margaret reflected, going back to the much-cheered Emily, it was not in her nature to worry.

No, Mother never worried, or if she did, nobody ever knew it. Care, fatigue, responsibility, long years of busy days and broken nights had left their mark on her face; the old beauty that had been hers was chiseled to a softer outline now; but there was a contagious serenity in Mrs. Paget's smile, a clear steadiness in her calm eyes, and her forehead, beneath a plain sweep of hair, was untroubled and smooth.

The children's mother was a simple woman; so absorbed in the hourly problems attendant upon the housing and feeding of her husband and family that her own personal ambitions, if she had any, were quite lost sight of, and the actual outlines of her character were forgotten by everyone, herself included. If her busy day marched successfully to nightfall, if darkness found her husband reading in his big chair, the younger children sprawled safe and asleep in the shabby nursery, the older ones contented with books or games, the clothes sprinkled, the bread set, the kitchen dark and clean, Mrs. Paget asked no more of life. She would sit, her workbasket beside her, looking from one absorbed face to another, thinking perhaps of Julie's new dress, of Ted's impending siege with the dentist, or of the old bureau up in the attic that might be mended for Bruce's room. "Thank God we all have warm beds," she would say, when they all went upstairs, yawning and chilly.

She had married, at twenty, the man she loved, and had found him better than her dreams in many ways—"the best man in the world." For more than twenty years he

had been satisfied to work diligently
behind a desk and to carry home his salary
envelope twice a month. Daddy was steady,
a hard worker and so gentle with the children. He delighted in Mrs. Paget's simple,
hearty meals and praised her in his own
quiet way. "God bless him," Mrs. Paget
would pray, looking from her kitchen
window to the garden where he trained the
pea vines, with the children's yellow heads
bobbing about him.

She welcomed the fast-coming babies as
gifts from God, marveled over their tiny
perfectness, dreamed over the soft, relaxed
little forms with a heart almost too full for
prayer. She was, in a word, old-fashioned,
hopelessly out of the modern current of
thoughts and events. She secretly regarded
her children as marvelous treasures, even
while she laughed down their youthful
conceit and punished their naughtiness.

Thinking a little of all these things, as a
girl with her own wifehood and mother-

hood all before her does think, Margaret went back to her hot luncheon. One o'clock found her at her desk, refreshed in spirit and much fortified in body. The room was well aired, and a reinforced fire roared in the little stove. One of the children had brought her a spray of pine, and the spicy fragrance of it reminded her that Christmas vacation was near; her mind was pleasantly busy with anticipation of the play that the Pagets always wrote and performed some time during the holidays, and with the New Year's costume dance at the Hall, and a dozen lesser festivities.

Suddenly, in the midst of a droning spelling lesson, there was a jarring interruption. From the world outside came a child's shrill screaming, which was instantly drowned by a chorus of frightened voices, and in the schoolroom below her own Margaret heard a thundering rush of feet and answering screams. With a suffocating terror at her heart she ran to the window, followed by every child in the room.

The rain had stopped now, and the sky showed a pale, cold, yellow light low in the west. At the schoolhouse gate an immense limousine car had come to a stop. The driver, his face alone visible between a great leather coat and visored leather cap, was talking unheard above the din. A tall woman, completely enveloped in furs, had evidently jumped from the limousine, and now held in her arms what made Margaret's heart turn sick and cold—the limp figure of a small girl.

About these central figures there surged the terrified crying of small children of the just-dismissed primer class, and in the half moment that Margaret watched, Mrs. Porter, white and shaking, and another teacher, Ethel Elliot, an always excitable girl, who was now sobbing and chattering hysterically, ran out from the school, each followed by her own class of crowding and excited girls.

With one horrified exclamation, Margaret ran downstairs and out to the gate. Mrs. Porter caught at her arm as she passed her in the path.

"God help us, Margaret! It's poor little Dorothy Scott!" she cried. "They've killed her. The car went completely over her!"

"Oh, Margaret, don't go near, oh, how can you!" screamed Miss Elliot. "Oh, and she's all they have! Who'll tell her mother?"

With astonishing ease, for the children gladly recognized authority, Margaret pushed through the group to the motor-car.

"Stop screaming—stop that shouting at once—keep still, every one of you!" she said firmly, shaking various shoulders as she went with such good effect that the voice of the woman in the furs could be heard by the time Margaret reached her.

"I don't think she's badly hurt!" said the woman, nervously and eagerly. She was evidently badly shaken, and was very white. "Do quiet them, can't you?" she said, with a sort of apprehensive impatience. "Can't we take her somewhere and get a doctor? Can't we get out of this?"

Margaret took the child into her own arms. Little Dorothy roared afresh, but to Margaret's unspeakable relief she twisted about and locked her arms tightly about the loved teacher's neck. The other woman watched them anxiously.

"That blood on her frock's just a nosebleed," she said, "but I think the car went over her! I assure you we were running very slowly. How it happened—! But I don't think she was struck."

"Nosebleed!" Margaret echoed, with a great breath. "No," she said quietly, over the agitated little head, "I don't think she's much hurt. We'll take her in. Now, look here, children," she added loudly to the assembled pupils of the Weston Grammar School, "I want every one of you children to go back to your schoolrooms; do you understand? Dorothy has had a bad scare, but she's got no broken bones, and we're going to have a doctor see that she's all right. I want you to see how quiet you can be. Mrs. Porter, may my class go into your room a little while?"

"Certainly," said Mrs. Porter, eager to cooperate and much relieved to have her share of the episode take this form. "Form lines, children," she added calmly.

"Ted," said Margaret to her own small brother, who had edged closer to her than any boy unprivileged by relationship dared, "will you go down the street and ask old Doctor Potts to come here? Then go tell Dorothy's mother that Dorothy has had a little bump, and that Miss Paget says she's all right, but that she'd like her mother to come for her."

"Sure I will, Mark!" Theodore responded enthusiastically, departing on a run.

"Mama!" sobbed the little sufferer at this point, hearing a familiar word.

"Yes, darling, you want Mama, don't

you?" Margaret said soothingly, as she started with her burden up the schoolhouse steps. "What were you doing, Dorothy," she went on pleasantly, "to get under that big car?"

"I dropped my ball!" wailed the small girl, her tears beginning afresh, "and it rolled and rolled. And I didn't see the automobile, and I didn't see it! And I fell down and b-b-bumped my nose!"

"Well, I should think you did!" Margaret said, laughing. "Mother won't know you at all with such a muddy face and such a muddy apron!"

Dorothy laughed a little shakily at this, and several other little girls, passing in orderly file, laughed heartily. Margaret crossed the lines of children to the room where they played and ate their lunches on wet days. She shut herself in with the child and the fur-clad lady.

"Now you're all right!" said Margaret gaily. And Dorothy was presently comfortable in a big chair, wrapped in a rug from the motor-car, with her face washed, and her head dropped languidly back against her chair, as became an interesting invalid. The Irish janitor was facetious as he replenished the fire, and made her laugh again. Margaret gave her a numerical chart to play with, and saw with satisfaction that the little head was bent interestedly over it.

Quiet fell over the school; the muffled sound of lessons recited in concert presently reached them. Theodore returned, reporting that the doctor would come as soon as he could and that Dorothy's mother was away at a card-party, but that Dorothy's "girl" would come for her as soon as the bread was out of the oven. There was nothing to do but wait.

"It seems a miracle," said the strange lady, in a low tone, when she and Margaret were alone again with the child. "But I don't believe she was scratched!"

"I don't think so," Margaret agreed.

"Mother says no child who can cry is very badly hurt."

"They made such a horrible noise," said the other, sighing wearily. She passed a white hand, with one or two blazing great stones upon it, across her forehead. Margaret had leisure now to notice that by all signs this was a very great lady indeed. The quality of her furs, the glimpse of her gown that the loosened coat showed, her rings, and most of all the tones of her voice, the authority of her manner, the well-groomed hair and skin and hands, all marked the thoroughbred.

"Do you know you managed that situation very cleverly just now?" said the lady, with a keen glance that made Margaret color. "One has such a dread of the crowd, just public sentiment, you know. Some officious bystander calls the police, they crowd against your driver, perhaps a brick gets thrown. We had an experience in England once—" She paused, then interrupted herself. "But I don't know your name?" she said brightly.

Margaret supplied it, and was led to talk a little of her own people.

"Seven of you, eh? Seven's too many," said the visitor, with the assurance that Margaret was to learn characterized her. "I've two myself, two girls," she went on. "I wanted a boy, but they're nice girls. And you've six brothers and sisters? Are they all as handsome as you and this Teddy of yours? And why do you like teaching?"

"Why do I like it?" Margaret echoed, enjoying these confidences and the unusual experience of sitting idle in mid-afternoon. "I don't."

"I see. But then why don't you come down to New York and do something else?" the other woman asked.

"I'm needed at home, and I don't know anyone there," Margaret said simply.

"I see," the lady said again thoughtfully. There was a pause. Then the same speaker said reminiscently, "I taught school once for three months when I was a girl, to show my father I could support myself."

"I've taught for four years," Margaret said.

"Well, if you ever want to try something else—there are such lots of fascinating things a girl can do now—be sure you come and see me about it," the stranger said. "I am Mrs. Carr-Boldt of New York."

Margaret's amazed eyes flashed to Mrs. Carr-Boldt's face; her cheeks crimsoned. "Mrs. Carr-Boldt!" she echoed blankly.

"Why not?" smiled the lady, not at all displeased.

"Why," stammered Margaret, laughing and rosy, "why, nothing—only I never dreamed who you were!" she finished, a little confused.

And indeed it never afterward seemed to her anything short of a miracle that brought the New York society woman— famed on two continents and from ocean to ocean for her jewels, her entertainments, her gowns, her establishments—into a Weston schoolroom and into Margaret Paget's life.

"I was on my way to New York now," said Mrs. Carr-Boldt.

"I don't see why you should be delayed," Margaret said, glad to be able to speak normally, with such a fast-beating and pleasantly excited heart. "I'm sure Dorothy's all right."

"Oh, I'd rather wait. I like my company," said the other. And Margaret decided in that instant that there never was a more deservedly admired and copied and quoted woman.

Presently their chat was interrupted by the tramp of the departing school children; the other teachers peeped in, were reassured, and went their ways. Then came the doctor, to pronounce the entirely cheerful Dorothy unhurt and to bestow upon her some hoarhound drops. Mrs. Carr-Boldt settled at once with the doctor, and when

Margaret saw the size of the bill that was pressed into his hand, she realized that she had done her old friend a good turn.

"Use it up on your poor people," said Mrs. Carr-Boldt over his protestations; and when he had gone, and Dorothy's "girl" appeared, she tipped that worthy and amazed servant, after promising Dorothy a big doll from a New York shop, and sent the child and maid home in the motor-car.

"I hope this hasn't upset your plans," Margaret said, as they stood waiting in the doorway. It was nearly five o'clock; the school was empty and silent.

"No, not exactly. I had hoped to get home for dinner. But I think I'll get Woolcock to take me back to Dayton; I've some very dear friends there who'll give me a cup of tea. Then I'll come back this way and get home by ten, I should think, for a late supper." Then, as the limousine appeared, Mrs. Carr-Boldt took both Margaret's hands in hers and said, "And now good-bye, my dear girl. I've got your address, and I'm going to send you something pretty to remember me by. You saved me from I don't know what annoyance and publicity. And don't forget that when you come to New York, I'm going to help you meet the people you want to, and give you a start if I can. You're far too clever and good-looking to waste your life down here. Good-bye!"

"Good-bye!" Margaret said, her cheeks brilliant, her head awhirl.

She stood unmindful of the chilly evening air, watching the great motor-car wheel and slip into the gloom. The rain was over; a dying wind moaned mysteriously through the dusk. Margaret went slowly upstairs, pinned on her hat, and buttoned her long coat snugly about her. She locked the schoolroom door, and, turning the corner, plunged her hands into her pockets, and faced the wind bravely. Deepening darkness and coldness were about her, but she felt surrounded by the warmth and brightness of her dreams. She saw the brilliant streets of a big city, the carriages and motor-cars coming and going, the idle, lovely women in their sumptuous gowns and hats. These things were real, near—almost attainable—tonight.

"Mrs. Carr-Boldt!" Margaret said, "the darling! I wonder if I'll ever see her again?"

CHAPTER II

Life in the shabby, commonplace house that sheltered the Paget family sometimes really did seem to proceed, as Margaret had suggested, in a long chain of violent shocks, narrow escapes, and closely averted catastrophes. No sooner was Duncan's rash pronounced not to be scarlet fever than Robert swallowed a penny, or Beck set fire to the dining room wastebasket, or Dad foresaw the immediate failure of the Weston Home Savings Bank and the inevitable loss of his position there. Sometimes there was a paternal reaction because Bruce liked to murmur vaguely of "dandy chances in Manila," or because Julie, pretty, excitable

and sixteen, had an occasional dose of
stage fever, and would stammer desper-
ately between convulsive sobs that she
wasn't half as much afraid of "the terrible
temptations of life" as she was afraid of
dying a poky old maid in Weston. In short,
the home was crowded, the Pagets were
poor, and every one of the seven children
possessed a spirited and distinct personal-
ity. Growing ambitions made the Weston
horizon seem narrow and mean, and the
young eyes that could not see beyond tomorrow were often wet with obstinate tears.

They all loved each other, and life
usually went by in utter harmony, the children contented over games and stories on
the hearthrug in the winter evenings, Julie
singing in the morning sunlight, as she
filled the vases from the marguerite
bushes on the lawn. But there were other
times when to the dreamy, studious
Margaret the home circle seemed all
discord, all dimness and threadbareness;

the struggle for ease and beauty and refinement seemed hopeless and overwhelming. In these times she would find herself staring thoughtfully at her mother's face, bent over the mending basket, or her eyes would leave the chessboard that held her father's attentions so closely, and move from his bald spot with its encircling crown of fluffy gray, to his rosy face with its kind, intent blue eyes and the little lines about his mouth that his moustache didn't hide—with a half-formed question in her heart. What hadn't they done, these dearest people, to be always struggling, always tired? Why were they content to be eternally harassed by plumber's bills and dentist's bills and shoes that would wear out and schoolbooks that must be bought? Why weren't they holding their place in Weston society, the place to which they were entitled by right of the Quincy grandfather and the uncles who were judges?

And in answer Margaret came despondently to the decision, "If you have children, you never have anything else!" How could mother keep up with her friends, when for some fifteen years she had been far too busy to put on a dainty gown in the afternoon and serve a hospitable cup of tea on the east porch? Mother was buttering bread for supper then, opening little beds and laying out little nightgowns, starting Ted off for the milk, washing small hands and faces, soothing bumps and binding cuts, admonishing, praising, directing. Mother was only too glad to sink gratefully into her rocker after dinner. Gradually, the fine friends had dropped away, and, except for their small church circle, the social life of Weston flowed smoothly on without the Pagets.

But when Margaret began to grow up, she grasped the situation with all the keenness of a restless and ambitious nature. Weston, detested Weston, it must apparently be. Very well, she would make the best of Weston. Margaret called on her mother's old friends; she was tireless in charming little attentions. Her own first socials had not been successful; she and Bruce were not good dancers, and Margaret had felt awkward in her plain gowns. When Julie's social days came along, Margaret saw to it that everything was made much easier. She planned social evenings at home and exhausted herself preparing for them, that Julie might know the "right people." To her mother all people were alike, if they were kind and not vulgar; Margaret felt differently. It was a matter of the greatest satisfaction to her when Julie blossomed into a fluffy-haired butterfly, tremendously popular in spite of much-cleaned slippers and often-pressed frocks. Margaret arranged Christmas theatricals, May picnics, Fourth of July gatherings. She never failed Bruce when this dearest brother wanted her company; she was, as Mrs. Paget told her over and over, "the sweetest daughter any woman ever had." But deep in her heart, Margaret knew moods of distaste and restlessness. The struggle did not seem worth the making; the odds against her seemed too great.

Still dreaming in the winter dark, she went through the home gate and up the porch steps of the roomy old house that had been built in the era of scalloped and pointed shingles, of colored glass embellishments around the window panes, of perforated scroll work and wooden railings in Grecian designs. A mass of wet overshoes lay on the porch, and two or three of the weather-stained porch rockers swayed under the weight of spread wet raincoats. Two opened umbrellas wheeled in the current of air that came around the house; the porch ran water. While Margaret was adding her own rainy-day equipment to the others, a golden-brown setter, one ecstatic wriggle from nose to tail, flashed into view, and came fawning to her feet.

"Hello, Bran!" Margaret said, propping herself against the house with one hand, while she pulled at a tight overshoe. "Hello, old fellow! Well, did they lock you out?"

She let herself and a freezing gust of air into the dark hall, groping to the hat-rack for matches. While she was lighting the gas, a very pretty girl of sixteen, with crimson cheeks and tumbled soft dark hair, came to the dining room door. This was her sister Julie, Margaret's roommate and warmest admirer, and for the last year or two her inseparable companion. Julie had her finger in a book, but now she closed it, and said affectionately between her yawns, "Come in here, darling! You must be dead."

"Don't let Bran in," cried some one from upstairs.

"He is in, Mother!" Margaret called back, and Rebecca and the three small boys— Theodore, the four-year-old baby, Robert, and Duncan, a grave little lad of seven—all rushed out of the dining room together, shouting as they fell on the delighted dog, "Aw, leave him in! Aw, leave the poor little feller in! Come on, Bran, come on, old feller! Leave him in, Mark, can't we?"

Kissing and hugging the dog and stumbling over each other and over him, they went back to the dining room, which was warm and stuffy. A coal fire was burning low in the grate, the window panes were beaded, and the little boys had marked their initials in the steam. They had also pushed the fringed table-cover almost off and scattered the contents of a box of "Lotto" over the scarred walnut top. The room was shabby, but comfortable. The Brussels carpet was worn thin, the chairs were of several different woods and patterns, and the old black walnut sideboard was battered and chipped. Julie and Margaret had established a tea table in the bay window, and had embroidered a lovely cover for the wide couch and the armchairs by the fire. Margaret dropped wearily into one of these, and the dark-eyed Julie hung over her with little affectionate attentions. The children returned to their game.

"Well, what a time you had with little Dolly Scott!" said Julie sympathetically. "Ted's been getting it all mixed up. Tell us about it. Poor old Mark, you're beat, aren't you? Would you like a cup of tea?"

"Love it!" Margaret said, a little surprised, for this luxury was not common.

"And toast!" said Theodore, enthusiastically.

"No, no—no tea!" said Mrs. Paget, coming in at this point with some sewing in her hands. "Don't spoil your dinner now, Mark dear; tea doesn't do you any good. And I think Blanche is saving the cream for an apple tapioca. Theodore, Mother wants you to go right downstairs for some coal, dear. And, Julie, you'd better start your table; it's close to six. Put up the game, please, Rebecca!"

There was general protest. Duncan, it seemed, needed only "two more" to win.

Little Robert, who was benevolently allowed by the other children to play the game exactly as he pleased, screamed delightedly that he needed only one more, and showed a card upon which even the blank spaces were lavishly covered with glass. He was generously conceded the victory and kissed by Rebecca and Julie as he made his way to his mother's lap.

"Why, this can't be Robert Paget!" exclaimed Mrs. Paget, putting aside her sewing to gather him in her arms. "Not this great, big boy!"

"Yes, I am!" the little fellow asserted joyously, dodging her kisses.

"Good to get home!" Margaret said luxuriously.

"You must sleep late in the morning," her mother commanded affectionately.

"Yes, because you have to be fresh for the party Monday!" exulted Julie. She had flung a white cloth over the long table and was putting the ringed napkins down with rapid bangs. "And New Year's Eve's the dance!" she went on buoyantly.

"Rebecca, ask Blanche if she needs me," called Mother over Robert's curly head.

"You'd go perfectly crazy about her, Ju. She's the most fascinating and the most unaffected woman!" Margaret was full of the day's real event.

Rebecca reported, "Blanche theth no, Mother, unleth you want to make thome cream gravy for the chopth!"

"And, Mark, Eleanor asked if Bruce and you and I weren't going as Pierrot and Peirettes; she's simply crazy to find out." This was Julie again; and then Margaret said coaxingly, "Do make cream gravy for Bruce, Mother. Give Baby to me!"

"Well, I think I will; there's milk," Mrs. Paget conceded, rising. "Put Bran out, Teddy; or put him in the laundry if you want to, while we have dinner." Margaret presently followed her mother into the kitchen, stopping in a crowded passageway to tie an apron over her gown.

"Bruce come in yet?" she asked in a low voice.

Her mother flashed her a sympathetic look. "I don't believe he's coming, Mark."

"Isn't! Oh, Mother! Oh, Mother, does he feel so badly about Betty?"

"I suppose so," Mrs. Paget went on with her bread cutting.

"But, Mother, did he really expect to marry Betty Forsythe?"

"I don't know why not, Mark. She's a sweet little thing, and Bruce has always admired her."

"But, Mother—" Margaret was a little at a loss. "We don't seem old enough to really be getting married!" she said, a little lamely.

"Brucie came in about half-past five, and said he was going over to Richie's," Mrs. Paget said with a sigh.

"In all this rain—that long walk!" Margaret cried, as she filled a long wicker basket with sliced bread.

"I think an evening of work with Richie will do him a world of good," said his mother. There was a pause. "There's Dad. I'll go in," she said as the front door slammed.

Margaret went in too, to kiss her father, a gray-haired man close to fifty, who had taken his chair at the head of the table by the fire. Mrs. Paget was anxious to be assured that his shoulders and shoes were not damp.

"But your hands are icy, dear," she said, as she set down a smoking tureen before her place at the table. "Come, have your nice hot soup. Pass that to Dad, Becky, and light the other gas. What sort of a day?"

"It was a hard day," said Mr. Paget, but his face brightened at his wife's concern and at the sight of his children gathering around the table. "Where's Bruce?" he asked. "Surely he hasn't forgotten what time we have dinner!"

"Bruce is going to have supper with Richie Williams," replied Mrs. Paget, serenely. "They'll get out their blueprints afterward and have a good evening's work. Fill the glasses before you sit down, please, Ju. Come, Ted—put that back on the mantel. Tell Daddy about what happened today, Mark—"

They all drew up their chairs. Robert, recently graduated from a high chair, was propped upon *The Officers of the Civil War* and *Household Book of Verse*. Julie tied on his bib and kissed the back of his fat little neck before she slipped into her own seat. The mother sat between Ted and Duncan, for reasons that immediately became obvious. Margaret sat by her father and attended to his needs, telling him all about the day, and laying her pretty slim hand over his as it rested beside his plate. Each head around the table bowed as father prayed a simple blessing, giving thanks for the meal and his family. Then, with happy chatter, plates were piled with food and the weariness of the long day began to slip away. The chops and cream gravy, as well as a mountain of baked potatoes and various vegetables were under discussion, when everyone stopped short in surprise at hearing the doorbell ring.

"Who—?" said Margaret, turning puzzled brows to her mother, and "I'm sure I—" her mother answered, shaking her head. Ted was heard to mutter uneasily that maybe it was old Pembroke, mad because the fellers had soaked his old skate with snowballs; Julie dimpled and said, "Maybe it's flowers!" Robert shouted, "Bakeryman!" more because he had recently acquired the word than because of any conviction on the subject. In the end Julie went to the door, with the four children in her wake. When she came back, she looked bewildered, and the children a little alarmed.

"It's—it's Mrs. Carr-Boldt, Mother," said Julie. "Well, don't leave her standing there in the cold, dear!" Mrs. Paget said, rising quickly to go into the hall. Margaret, her heart thumping with an unanalyzed premonition of something pleasant, and nervous, too, for the hospitality of the Pagets, followed her. So they were all presently crowded into the hall, Mrs. Paget all hospitality, Margaret full of a fear she would have denied that her mother would not be equal to the occasion.

The visitor, fur-clad, rain-spattered—for it was raining again—and beaming, stretched a hand to Mrs. Paget.

"You're Mrs. Paget, of course—this is an awful hour to interrupt you," she said in her big, easy way, "and there's my Miss Paget— how do you do? But you see I must get up to town tonight—in this door? I can see perfectly, thank you—and I did want a little talk with you and Mr. Paget first. Now, what a shame!"—for the gas, lighted by Theodore at this point, revealed Duncan's bib and the napkins some of the others were still carrying. "I've interrupted your dinner! Won't you let me wait here until—"

"Perhaps—if you haven't had your supper—you will have some with us," said Mrs. Paget a little uncertainly. Margaret inwardly shuddered, but Mrs. Carr-Boldt was gracious.

"Mrs. Paget, that's charming of you," she said, "but I had tea at Dayton and mustn't lose another moment. I shan't dine until I get home. I'm the busiest woman in the world, you know. Now, it won't take me two minutes—"

She was seated now, her hands still deep in her muff, for the parlor was freezing cold. Mrs. Paget, with a rather bewildered look, called, "Father, can you come here a moment?" and sat down, too. Mr. Paget brushed off his well worn house coat, and joined his wife.

"You can run back to your dinners," Mother said to the children. "Take them, Julie. Mark, dear, will you serve the pudding?" They all filed dutifully out of the room, and Margaret, excited and curious, continued a meal that might have been of sawdust and sand for all she knew.

The young people sat almost without speaking, listening to the indistinguishable murmur from the adjoining room, and smiling mysteriously at each other. Then Margaret was called, and went back as far as the dining room door before coming back to put her napkin uncertainly down at her place. She hesitated, arranged her gown carefully, and finally went out again. They heard her voice in the parlor . . . questioning . . . laughing . . . .

Presently the low murmur broke into audible farewells; chairs were pushed back; feet scraped in the hall.

"Good night, then!" said Mrs. Carr-Boldt's clear tones, "and so sorry to have—Good night, Mr. Paget!—Oh, thank you—but I'm well wrapped. Thank you! Good night, dear! I'll wait to hear from you."

And then came the honking of the motor-car, and a great swish where it grazed a wet bush near the house. Somebody lowered the gas in the hall, and Mrs. Paget's voice said regretfully, "I wish we had a fire in the parlor—just one of the times!—but there's no help for it." They all came in, Margaret flushed, starry-eyed; her father and mother a little serious. The three blinked at the brighter light and fell upon the cooling chops as if eating were the important business of the moment.

"We waited for the pudding," said Julie. "What is it?"

"Well—" Mrs. Paget began, hesitatingly, looking at her husband. Mr. Paget briskly continued with an air of making further talk unnecessary, "Mrs. Carr-Boldt needs a secretary and helper for her children, and she has offered your sister Margaret the position. That's the whole affair in a nutshell. Your mother and I will consider the matter, but I want to say here and now that I don't want any child of mine to make this a matter of general gossip in the neighborhood."

"Wants Margaret!" gasped Julie, unaffected—so astonishing was the news—by her father's sternness. "Oh, Mother! Oh, Mark! Oh, you lucky thing! When is she coming down here?"

"She isn't coming down here—she wants Mark to go to her—that's it," said her mother.

"Mark—in New York!" shrilled Theodore. Julie got up to rush around the table and kiss her sister; the younger children laughed and shouted.

"There is no occasion for all this," said Mr. Paget, sipping a fresh cup of tea. "Quiet down, children. I see nothing very extraordinary in the matter. This woman needs a secretary and companion for her children, and she offered the position to Mark."

Father ended the discussion for the evening, and a few days later when the family had gathered for dinner, Mr. and Mrs. Paget announced their decision to send Margaret to New York to serve the Carr-Boldt family.

"Oh, if I only can do it!" burst from Margaret, with a little childish gasp. She was sitting back from the table, twisted about so that she sat sideways, her hands clasped about the top of her chair back. Her soft hair was loosened about her face, her dark eyes aflame.

"Why, I think it's simply extraordinary!" exulted the generous little sister. "Oh, Mark, isn't this just the sort of thing you would have wished to happen! With your beautiful handwriting, you'll be just invaluable to her! And your German—and I'll bet you'll just have them all adoring you—!"

"Lenox, she said," Margaret went on dazedly, "and Europe, and traveling everywhere! And a hundred dollars a month, and nothing to spend it on, so I can still help out here! Why, it—I can't believe it!"— she looked from one smiling interested face to another, and suddenly her radiance underwent a quick eclipse. Her lip trembled, and she tried to laugh as she pushed her chair back and ran to the arms her mother opened. "Oh, Mother!" sobbed Margaret, clinging there, "Do you want me to go—shall I go? I've always been so happy here, and I feel so ashamed of being discontented—and I don't deserve a thing like this to happen to me!"

"Why, bless your heart!" said Mrs. Paget, tenderly, "Of course you'll go!"

"Oh, you silly! I'll never speak to you again if you don't!" laughed Julie through sympathetic tears.

Theodore and Duncan immediately burst into a radiant reminiscence of their one brief visit to New York; Rebecca was heard to murmur that she would "vithet Mark thome day;" and the baby, tugging at his mother's elbow, asked sympathetically if Mark was naughty—and was caught between his sister's and his mother's arms and kissed by them both.

Mr. Paget, picking up the family Bible from the sideboard, took an armchair by the fire, and, clearing his throat, he called the children to settle quietly around him for the evening's Bible reading and prayer. Mother took little Bob into her lap and glanced round at the others as they pulled chairs closer to Father's or sat down on the floor at his feet. She smiled at Margaret's attempt to blink the stars out of her eyes and listen attentively as Father read from the Psalms. When he turned to the thirty-first Proverb, Father smiled at Mother, then glanced at Margaret. "Who can find a virtuous woman? For her price is far above rubies." Father closed the Bible and placed his hand on Margaret's, which rested on the arm of his chair.

"Wherever you go, my dear," he said, "I want you always to remember that a virtuous woman is precious in the sight of God. Fame, fortune, and education do not alone make a woman." He smiled at Mother. "A true woman can serve in a palace or a cottage with contentment and joy."

Mother took Margaret's other hand and pressed it tightly. The younger children looked on with awe, feeling that the occasion was a solemn one and not fully understanding why. Father bent his head and prayed fervently for Margaret and the work she would undertake, asking the blessing of the Almighty to guide and protect his girl. After a husky "Amen," Margaret wiped tears from her eyes and smiled up at her parents, who were surreptitiously wiping tears from their own faces.

Dinner concluded, the youngest children were hustled up to bed and tucked warmly under their quilts before Mother, Margaret, Julie, and Father settled around the fire again. Margaret's mood was pensive. "Suppose I don't suit?" she asked suddenly, sitting back on her heels with her arms laid across her mother's lap.

"Oh, you'll suit," said Julie confidently;

and Mrs. Paget smoothed the girl's hair back and said affectionately, "I don't think she'll find many girls like you for the asking, Mark!"

"Reading English lessons with the two little girls," said Margaret, dreamily, "and answering notes and invitations. And keeping books and dinner lists. You know, Mother—doesn't it sound like an English story?" Margaret stopped in the middle of an ecstatic wriggle. "Mother, will you and Father pray every day that I succeed?" she asked solemnly.

"You know we will, Mark dear. You just be your own dear, simple self," her mother advised. "January!" she added with a great sigh. "It's the first break, isn't it, Father? Think of us trying to get along without our Mark!"

"January!" Julie was instantly alert. "Why, but you'll need all sorts of clothes!"

"Oh, she says there's a sewing woman always in the house," Margaret said, almost embarrassed by the still-unfolding advantages of the proposition. "I can have her do whatever's left over."

By the light of the dying fire, they talked, yawned, made a pretense of breaking up, talked, and yawned again. The room grew chilly. Bruce presently came in and was given the news and marveled in his turn. Bruce and Margaret had talked of their ambitions a hundred times: of the day when he might enter college and when she might find the leisure and beauty in life for which her heart hungered. Now, as she sat with his arm about her and her head on his shoulder, he said with generous satisfaction, "It was coming to you, Mark; I'm happy for you. I hope it's everything you've wanted."

At midnight, loitering upstairs, cold and yawning, Margaret kissed her mother and father quietly, with whispered brief good-nights. But Julie, lying warm and snug in bed half an hour later, had a last word, "You know, Mark, I think I'm as happy as you are—no, I'm not generous at all! It's just that it makes me feel that things do come your way finally, if you wait long enough, and that we aren't the only family in town that never has anything decent happen to it! . . . I'll miss you awfully, Mark, darling! . . . Mark, do you suppose Mother'd let me take this bed out and just have a big couch in here? It would make the room seem so much bigger. And then I could have the girls come up here. Think of you—*you*—going abroad! I'd simply die! I can't wait to tell Betty! . . . We've had this room a long time together, haven't we, Mark? Ever since Grandma died. Do you remember her canary, that Teddy hit with a plate? . . . I'm going to miss you terribly, Mark. But we'll write. . . ."

CHAPTER III

In the days that followed, the miracle came to be accepted by all Weston, which was much excited for a day or two over this honor done a favorite daughter, and by all the Pagets—except Margaret. Margaret went through the hours in her old, quiet manner, a little more tender and gentle perhaps than she had been; but her heart never beat normally, and she lay awake at night and early in the morning, thinking, thinking, thinking. She tried to realize that it was in her honor that a farewell tea was planned at the club; it was for her that her fellow teachers were planning a good-bye luncheon; it was really she—Margaret Paget—

whose voice said on the telephone a dozen times a day, "On the fourteenth—Oh, do I? I don't feel calm! Can't you try to come in— I do want to see you before I go!" She dutifully repeated Bruce's careful directions: she was to give her check to an expressman, and her suitcase to a red-cap; the expressman would probably charge fifty cents, the red-cap was to have no more than fifteen. And she was to tell the latter to put her into a taxicab.

"I'll remember," Margaret assured him gratefully, but with a sense of unreality pressing almost painfully upon her. One of a million ordinary school teachers in a million little towns—and this marvel had befallen her!

The night of the Paget's Christmas play came, a night full of laughter and triumph; and marked for Margaret by the little parting gifts that were slipped into her hands, and by the warm good wishes that were murmured, not always steadily, by this old friend and that. When the time came to distribute plates and paper napkins and great saucers of ice cream and sliced cake, Margaret was toasted in cold sweet lemonade. And drawing together to "harmonize" more perfectly, the circle about her touched their glasses while they sang, "For she's a jolly good fellow." Later, when the little supper was almost over, Ethel Elliot, leaning over to lay her hand on Margaret's, began in her rich contralto, "When other lips and other hearts . . ." and as they all went seriously through the two verses, they stood up, one by one, and linked arms; the little circle, affectionate and admiring, that had bounded Margaret's friendships until now.

Then Christmas came, with a dark, freezing walk to the pine-spiced and candle-lighted early service in the little church, and a quicker walk home, chilled and happy and hungry, to a riotous Christmas breakfast and a littered breakfast table. The New Year came, with a dance and revel, and the Pagets took one of their long tramps through the snowy afternoon, and came back hungry for a big dinner.

Then there was dressmaking—Mrs. Schmidt in command, Mrs. Paget tireless at the machine, Julie all eager interest. Margaret, patiently standing to be fitted, conscious of the icy, wet touch of Mrs. Schmidt's red fingers on her bare arms, dreamily acquiescent as to buttons or hooks, was totally absent in spirit.

A trunk came, Mr. Paget very anxious that the keys should not be "fooled with" by the children. Margaret's mother packed this trunk scientifically. "No, now the shoes, Mark—now that heavy skirt," she would say. "Run get mother some more tissue paper, Beck. You'll have to leave the big cape, dear, and you can send for it if you need it. Now the blue dress, Ju. I think that dyed so prettily, just the thing for mornings. And here's your prayer book in the tray, dear; if you go Saturday, you'll want it first thing in the morning. See, I'll put a fresh handkerchief in it—"

Margaret, relaxed and idle in a rocker with Duncan in her lap busily playing with her locket, would say over and over, "You're all such angels—I'll never forget it!" and wish that, knowing how sincerely she meant it, she could feel it a little more. Conversation languished in these days; mother and daughter feeling that time was too precious to waste speech on little things, and that their hearts were too full to touch upon the great change impending.

A night came when the Pagets went early upstairs, saying that, after all, it was not like people marrying and going to Russia; it was not like a real parting; it wasn't as if Mark couldn't come home again in four hours if anything went wrong at either end of the line. Margaret's heart was beating high and quick now; she tried to show some of the love and sorrow she felt under the hurry of her blood that made speech impossible. She went to her mother's door, slender and girlish in her white nightgown, to kiss her good-night again. Mrs. Paget's big arms went about her daughter. Margaret laid her head childishly on her mother's shoulder. Nothing of significance was said. Margaret whispered, "Mother, I love you!" Her mother said, "You were such a little thing, Mark, when I kissed you one day, without hugging you, and you said, 'Please, don't love me with just your heart!'" Then she added, "Did you and Julie get that extra blanket down today, dear? It's going to be very cold." Margaret nodded. "Good-night, little girl—" "Good-night, Mother—" Then there was Father's warm embrace and his hand fondly pinching her cheek before he gruffly bid her good-night.

That was the real farewell, for the next morning was all confusion. They dressed hurriedly, by chilly gas-light; clocks were compared, Rebecca's back buttoned; Duncan's overcoat jerked on; coffee drunk scalding hot as they stood about the kitchen table; bread barely tasted. They walked to the railway station on wet sidewalks, under a broken sky. Bruce, with Margaret's suitcase, in the lead. Weston was asleep in the gray morning after the storm. Far and near belated cocks were crowing.

A score of old friends met Margaret at the train; there were gifts, promises, good wishes. There came a moment when it was generally felt that the Pagets should be left alone now—the far whistle of the train beyond the bridge—the beginning of good-byes—a sudden filling of the mother's eyes that was belied by her smile. "Good-bye, sweetest—don't knock my hat off, baby dear! Beck, darling—Oh, Ju, do! Don't just say you will—start me a letter tonight. Everyone write to me! Good-bye, Dad, darling—all right, Bruce, I'll get right in! Good-bye!"

Then for the Pagets there was a walk
back to the empty disorder of the house;
Julie very talkative at her father's side;
Bruce walking far behind the others with
his mother—and the day's familiar
routine to be somehow gone through
without Margaret.

But for Margaret, settling herself
comfortably in the grateful warmth of the
train, and watching the uncertain early
sunshine brighten unfamiliar fields and
farmhouses, every brilliant possibility of
life seemed to be waiting. She tried to read,
to think, to pray, to stare steadily out of the
window; she could do nothing for more
than a moment at a time. Her thoughts
went backward and forward like a weaving
shuttle, "How good they've all been to me!
How grateful I am! Now if only, only, I can
make good!"

"Look out for the servants!" Julie, from
the depth of her sixteen-year-old wisdom
had warned her sister. "The governess will

hate you because she'll be afraid you'll cut
her out, and Mrs. Carr-Boldt's maid will be
a cat! They always are, in books."

Margaret had laughed at this advice, but
in her heart she rather believed it. Her new
work seemed so enchanting to her that it
was not easy to believe that she did not
stand in somebody's light. She was glad
that by a last-moment arrangement she
was to arrive at the Grand Central Station
at almost the same moment as Mrs. Carr-
Boldt herself, who was coming home from a
three-weeks' visit in the Middle West.
Margaret gave only half her attention to
the flying country that was beginning to
shape itself into streets and rows of houses.
All the last half-hour of the trip was
clouded by the nervous fear that she would
somehow fail to find Mrs. Carr-Boldt in the
confusion at the railroad terminal.

But happily enough the lady was found
without trouble, or rather Margaret was
found, felt an authoritative tap on her

shoulder, caught a breath of fresh violets and a glimpse of her patron's clear-skinned, resolute face. They whirled through wet, deserted streets; Mrs. Carr-Boldt gracious and talkative, Margaret nervously interested and amused.

Their wheels presently grated against a curb. A man in livery opened the limousine door. Margaret saw an immense stone mansion facing the park, climbed a dazzling flight of wide steps, and was in a great hall that faced an interior court, where there were Florentine marble benches and the great lifted leaves of palms. She was a little dazed by crowded impressions of height and spaciousness and richness and opening vistas: a great marble stairway, and a landing where there was an immense designed window in clear leaded glass; rugs, tapestries, mirrors, polished wood and great chairs with brocaded seats and carved dark backs. Two little girls, heavy, well-groomed little girls—one spectacled and good-natured looking, the other rather pretty, with a mass of fair hair—were coming down the stairs with an eager little German woman. They kissed their mother, much diverted by the mad rushes and leaps of the two white poodles who accompanied them.

"These are my babies, Miss Paget," said Mrs. Carr-Boldt. "This is Victoria, who's eleven, and Harriet, who's six. And these are Monsieur—"

"Monsieur Patou and Monsieur Mouche," said Victoria, introducing the dogs with entire ease of manner. The German woman said something forcibly, and Margaret understood the child's reply in that tongue, "Mamma won't blame you, Fräulein; Harriet and I wished them to come down!"

Presently they all went up in a luxuriously fitted little lift, Margaret being carried to the fourth floor to her own rooms, to which a little maid escorted her.

When the maid had gone, Margaret walked to the door and tried it, for no reason whatever; it was shut. Her heart was beating violently. She walked into the middle of the room and looked at herself in the mirror, laughed a little breathless laugh. Then she took off her hat carefully and went into the bedroom that was beyond her sitting room, and hung her hat in a fragrant white closet that was entirely and delightfully empty, and put her coat on a hanger, and her gloves and bag in the empty big top drawer of a great mahogany bureau. Then she went back to the mirror and looked hard at herself reflected in it; and laughed her little laugh again. "It's too good—it's too much!" she whispered.

She investigated her domain, after quelling a wild desire to sit down at the beautiful desk and try the new pens, the crystal inkwell, and the heavy paper with its severely engraved address, in a long letter to Mother.

There was a tiny upright piano in the sitting room, and at the fireplace a deep, thick rug, and an immense leather armchair. A clock in crystal and gold flanked by two crystal candlesticks had the centre of the mantlepiece. On the little round mahogany centre table was a lamp with a wonderful mosaic shade; a little bookcase was filled with books and magazines. Margaret went to one of the three windows and looked down upon the bare trees and the snow in the park, and upon the rumbling green omnibuses, all bathed in bright, chilly sunlight.

A mahogany door with a crystal knob opened into the bedroom, where there was a polished floor and more rugs and a gay rosy wallpaper, and a great bed with a lace cover. Beyond was a bathroom, all enamel, marble, glass and nickel-plate, with heavy monogrammed towels on the rack, three new little wash-cloths sealed in glazed paper, three new toothbrushes in paper cases, and a cake of famous English soap just out of its wrapper.

Over the whole little suite there brooded an exquisite order. Not a particle of dust broke the shining surfaces of the mahogany, not a fallen leaf lay under the great bowl of roses on the desk. Now and then the radiator clanked in the stillness; it was hard to believe in that warmth and silence that a cold winter wind was blowing outside, and that snow still lay on the ground.

Margaret, resting in the big chair, became thoughtful; presently she went into the bedroom and knelt down beside the bed.

"Oh, Lord, let me stay here," she prayed, her face in her hands. "I want so to stay— please make me a success and a help!"

Never was a prayer more generously answered. Miss Paget was an instant success. In something less than two months she became indispensable to Mrs.

Carr-Boldt and was a favorite with everyone, from the rather stolid, silent head of
the house down to the least of the maids.
She was so busy, so unaffected, so sympathetic, that her sudden rise in favor was
resented by no one. The butler told her his
troubles, the French maid darkly declared
that but for Miss Paget she would not for
one second r-r-remain! The children went
cheerfully even to the dentist with their
adored Miss Peggy; they soon preferred her
escort to matinee or zoo to that of any other
person. Margaret also escorted Mrs. Carr-
Boldt's mother, a magnificent old lady, on
shopping expeditions, and attended the
meetings of charity boards for Mrs. Carr-
Boldt. With notes and invitations, account
books and cheque books, dinner lists and
interviews with caterers, decorators and
florists, Margaret's time was full, but she
loved every minute of her work and gloried
in her increasing usefulness.

At first there were some dark days;

notably the dreadful one upon which
Margaret somehow—somewhere—dropped
the box containing the new hat she was
bringing home for Harriet, and kept the
little girl out in the cold afternoon air while
the motor made a fruitless trip back to the
milliner's. Harriet contracted a cold, and
Harriet's mother for the first time spoke
severely to Margaret. There was another
bad day when Margaret artlessly admitted
to Mrs. Pierre Polk on the telephone that
Mrs. Carr-Boldt was not engaged for
dinner that evening, thus obliging her
employer to snub the lady, or accept a
distasteful invitation to dine. And there
was a most uncomfortable occasion when
Mr. Carr-Boldt, not at all at his best, stumbled in upon his wife with some angry
observations meant for her ear alone; and
Margaret, busy with accounts in a window
recess, was, unknown to them both, a
distressed witness.

"Another time, Miss Paget," said Mrs.

Carr-Boldt coldly, upon Margaret's appearing scarlet-cheeked between the curtains, "don't oblige me to ascertain that you are not within hearing before feeling sure of privacy. Will you finish those bills upstairs, if you please?"

Margaret went upstairs with a burning heart, cast her bills haphazard on her own desk and flung herself, dry-eyed and furious, on the bed. She lay there for perhaps twenty minutes with her brain whirling. Finally rising, she brushed up her hair, straightened her collar, and full of tremendous resolve, stepped into her little sitting room, to find Mrs. Carr-Boldt in the big chair, serenely eyeing her.

"I'm sorry I spoke so, Peggy," said her employer generously. "But the truth is, I am not myself when—when Mr. Carr-Boldt—" The little hesitating appeal in her voice completely disarmed Margaret. In the end, the little episode cemented the rapidly growing friendship between the two women, Mrs. Carr-Boldt seeming to enjoy the relief of speaking rather freely of what was the one real trial in her life.

"My husband has always had too much money," she said, in her positive way. "At one time we were afraid that he would absolutely ruin his health by this—habit of his. His physician and I took him around the world—I left Victoria, just a baby, with my mother—and for two years he was never out of my sight. It has never been so bad since. You know yourself how reliable he usually is," she finished cheerfully, "unless some of the other men get hold of him!" Margaret returned her employer's smile, though she felt a piercing distaste at the thought of a grown man behaving in such a fashion. Father would certainly never have done so.

As the months went on Margaret came to admire her employer more and more. There was not an indolent impulse in Mrs. Carr-Boldt's entire composition. Smooth-haired, fresh-skinned, in spotless linen, she began the day at eight o'clock, full of energy and interest. She had daily sessions with butler and housekeeper, shopped with Margaret and the children, walked about her greenhouse or her country garden with her skirts pinned up, and had tulips potted and stonework continued. She was prominent in several clubs, a famous dinner-giver, she took a personal interest in all her servants, loved to settle their quarrels and have three or four of them up on the carpet at once, tearful and explanatory

Margaret kept for her a list of some two hundred friends, whose birthdays were to be marked with carefully selected gifts. She pleased Mrs. Carr-Boldt by her open amazement at the latter's vitality. The girl observed that her employer could not visit any institution without making a few vigorous suggestions as she went about; she accompanied her cheques to the organized charities—and her charity flowed only

through absolutely reliable channels—
with little friendly, advisory letters. She
liked the democratic attitude for herself,
even while promptly snubbing any such
tendency in children or friends, and told
Margaret that she only used her coat of
arms on house linen, stationery, and livery,
because her husband and mother liked it.
"It's of course rather nice to realize that one
comes from one of the oldest Colonial families," she would say. "The Carterets of
Maryland, you know. But it's all such bosh!"

And she urged Margaret to claim her
own right to family honors, "You're a
Quincy, my dear! Don't let that woman
intimidate you—she didn't remember that
her grandfather was a captain until her
husband made his money. And where the
family portraits came from I don't know,
but I think there's a man on Fourth Avenue
who does them!" she would say, or, "I know
all about Lilly Reynolds, Peggy. Her father
was as rich as she says, and I daresay the

crest is theirs. But ask her what her maternal grandmother did for a living, if you want to shut her up!" Other people she would condemn with a mere whispered, "Coal!" or "Patent bathtubs!" behind her fan, and it pleased her to tell people that her treasure of a secretary had the finest blood in the world in her veins. Margaret was much admired, and Margaret was her discovery, and she liked to emphasize her find.

Mrs. Carr-Boldt's mother, a tremulous, pompous old lady, unwittingly aided the impression by taking an immense fancy to Margaret, and by telling her few intimates and the older women among her daughter's friends that the girl was a perfect little thoroughbred. When the Carr-Boldts filled their house with the reckless and noisy company they occasionally affected, Mrs. Carteret would say majestically to Margaret, "You and I have nothing in common with this riff-raff, my dear!"

Summer came, and Margaret headed a happy letter "Bar Harbor." Two months later all Weston knew that Margaret Paget was going abroad for a year with those rich people and had written her mother from the Lusitania. Letters from London, from Germany, from Holland, from Russia, followed. "We are going to put the girls at school in Switzerland, and (ahem!) winter on the Riviera, and then Rome for Easter!" she wrote.

She was presently home again, chattering French and German to amuse her father, teaching Becky a little Italian song to match her little Italian costume.

"It's wonderful to me how you get along with all these rich people, Mark," said her mother, admiringly, during Margaret's home visit. Mrs. Paget was watering the dejected-looking side garden with a straggling length of hose; Margaret and Julie shelling peas on the side steps. Margaret laughed, coloring a little.

"Why, we're just as good as they are, Mother!"

Mrs. Paget drenched a dried little clump of carnations.

"We're as good," she admitted, "but we're not as rich or as traveled—we haven't the same ideas; we live in a different world."

"Oh, no we don't, Mother," Margaret said quickly. "Who are the Carr-Boldts, except for their money? Why, Mrs. Carteret—for all her family!—isn't half the aristocrat Grandma was! And you— you could be a Daughter of the Officers of the Revolution, Mother!"

"Why, Mark, I never heard that!" her mother protested, cleaning the sprinkler with a hairpin.

"Mother!" Julie said eagerly, "Great-grandfather Quincy!"

"Oh, Grandpa," said Mrs. Paget. "Yes, Grandpa was a paymaster. He was on Governor Hancock's staff. They used to call him 'Major.' But Mark—" she turned off the water, holding her skirts away from the combination of mud and dust underfoot, "that's a very silly way to talk, dear! It does no good to go back into the past and say that this one was a judge and that one a major; we must live our lives where we are, with what God has given."

Margaret had not lost a wholesome respect for her mother's opinion in the two years she had been away, but she had lived in a very different world and was full of new ideas.

"Mother, do you mean to tell me that if you and Dad hadn't had a perfect pack of children, and moved so much, and if Dad, say, had been in that oil deal that he said he wished he had the money for, and we still lived in the brick house, that you wouldn't be in every way the equal of Mrs. Carr-Boldt?"

"If you mean equal as far as money goes, Mark—no. We might have been well-to-do as country people go, I suppose—"

"Exactly!" said Margaret, "And you would have been as well off as dozens of the people who are going about in society this minute! It's the merest chance that we aren't rich. Just for instance: Father's father had twelve children, didn't he? And left them—how much was it? About three thousand dollars apiece—"

"And it was a Godsend, Mark, not chance," said her mother, reflectively.

"But suppose Dad had been the only child, Mother," Margaret persisted, "he would have had—"

"He would have had the whole thirty-six thousand dollars, I suppose, Mark."

"Or more," said Margaret, "for Grandfather Paget was presumably spending money on them all the time."

"Well, but Mark," said Mrs. Paget, laughing as at the vagaries of a small child, "Father Paget did have twelve children— and Daddy and I eight, wanting every one—" she sighed, as always, at the

thought of the little son who was gone—
"and there you are! You can't get away from
that, dear."

Margaret did not answer. But she
thought to herself that very few people
held Mother's views of this subject.

Mrs. Carr-Boldt's friends, for example,
did not accept increasing cares in this
contented fashion; their lives were ideally
pleasant and harmonious without the
complicated responsibilities of large families. They drifted from season to season
without care, always free, always gay,
always irreproachably gowned. In winter
there were daily meetings, for shopping, for
luncheon, bridge, or tea; summer was filled
with a score of country visits. There were
motor-trips for week-ends, dinners,
theatre, and the opera to fill the evenings,
German or singing lessons, manicure,
masseuse, and dressmaker to crowd the
morning hours all the year round.
Margaret learned from these exquisite,

fragrant creatures the art of being perpetually fresh and charming, learned their methods of caring for their own beauty, learned to love rare perfumes and powders, fine embroidered linen, and silk stockings. There was no particular strain upon her wardrobe now, nor upon her purse; she could be as dainty as she liked. She listened to the conversations that went on about her—sometimes critical or unconvinced; more often admiring; and as she listened she formed slowly but certainly her own viewpoint. She was not mercenary. She would not marry a man just for his money, she decided, but just as certainly she would not marry a man who could not give her a comfortable establishment and a position in society.

The man seemed in no hurry to appear; as a matter of fact, the men whom Margaret met were openly anxious to avoid marriage, even with the wealthy girls of their own set. Margaret was not concerned;

she was too happy to miss the romantic element; the men she saw were not of a type to inspire a sensible, busy, happy girl with any very deep feeling. And it was with generous and perfect satisfaction that she presently had news of Julie's happy engagement. Julie was to marry a young and popular doctor, the only child of one of Weston's most prominent families. The little sister's letter bubbled joyously with news.

"Harry's father is going to build us a little house on the big place, the darling," wrote Julie, "and we will stay with them until it is done. But in five years Harry says we will have a real honeymoon, in Europe! Think of going to Europe as a married woman. Mark, I wish you could see my ring; it is a beauty, but don't tell Mother I was silly enough to write about it!"

Margaret delightedly selected a little collection of things for Julie's trousseau. A pair of silk stockings, a scarf she never had worn, a lace petticoat, pink silk for a waist. Mrs. Carr-Boldt, coming in in the midst of these preparations, insisted upon adding so many other things from trunks and closets that Margaret was speechless with delight. Scarves, cobwebby silks in uncut lengths, embroidered lingerie still in the tissue paper of Paris shops, parasols, gloves and lengths of lace—she piled them all into Margaret's arms. Julie's trousseau was consequently quite the most beautiful Weston had ever seen; and the little sister's cloudless joy made the fortnight Margaret spent at home at the time of the wedding a very happy one. It was a time of rush and flurry, laughter and tears, of roses and girls in white gowns. But some ten days before the wedding, Julie and Margaret happened to be alone for a peaceful hour over their sewing, and fell to talking seriously.

"You see, our house will be small," said Julie, "but I don't care. We don't intend to stay in Weston all our lives. Don't breathe this to anyone, Mark, but if Harry does as well as he's doing now for two years, we'll rent the little house and go to Baltimore for a year for a special course. Then—you know he's devoted to Doctor McKim—he always calls him 'the chief'—then he thinks maybe McKim will work him into his practice. He's getting old, you know, and that means New York!"

"Oh, Ju—really!"

"I don't see why not," Julie said, dimpling. "Harry's crazy to do it. He says he doesn't propose to live and die in Weston. McKim could throw any amount of hospital practice his way, to begin with. And you know Harry'll have something; and the house will rent." Julie bubbled on, "I'm crazy to take one of those lovely old apartments on Washington Square and meet a few nice people, you know, and really make something of my life!"

"Mrs. Carr-Boldt and I will spin down for you every few days," Margaret said, falling readily in with the plan. "I'm glad you're not going to simply get into a rut the way some other girls have, cooking and babies and nothing else!" she said.

"I think that's an awful mistake," Julie said placidly. "Starting right is so important. I don't want to be a mere drudge like Ethel or Louise—they may like it. I don't! Of course, this isn't a matter to talk of," she went on, coloring a little. "I'd never breathe this to Mother! But it's perfectly absurd to pretend that girls don't discuss these things. I've talked to Betty and Louise—we all talk about it, you know. And Louise says they haven't had one free second since Buddy came. She can't keep one maid, and she says the idea of two maids eating three meals a day, whether she's home or not, makes her perfectly sick! Someone's got to be with him every single second, even now, when he's four, to see that he doesn't fall off something or put things in his mouth. And as Louise says, it means no more weekend trips; you can't go visiting overnight, you can't even go for a day's drive or a day on the beach, without extra clothes for the baby, a mosquito net and an umbrella for the baby—milk packed in ice for the baby—somebody's trying to get the baby to take his nap—it's awful! It would end our Baltimore plan, and that means New York, and New York means everything to Harry and me!" finished Julie, flattening a finished bit of embroidery on her knee and regarding it complacently.

"Well, I think you're right," Margaret approved. "Things are different now from what they were in Mother's day."

"And look at Mother," Julie said. "One long slavery! Life's too short to wear yourself out that way."

Mrs. Paget's sunny cheerfulness was shaken when the actual moment of parting with the exquisite, rose-hatted, gray-frocked Julie came; her face worked pitifully in its effort to smile; her tall figure, awkward in an unbecoming new silk, seemed to droop tenderly over the little clinging wife. Margaret, stirred by the sight of tears on her mother's face, stood with an arm about her when the bride and groom drove away in the afternoon sunshine.

"I'm going to stay with you until she gets back!" she reminded her mother.

"You know we've always wanted the girls to marry, Mother," urged Mr. Paget. "Julie's married a fine young man, and they have my blessing!" Father patted Mother's arm and lifted her chin to make her smile. Rebecca felt this a felicitous moment to ask if she and the boys could have the rest of the ice cream.

"Divide it evenly," said Mrs. Paget, wiping her eyes and smiling. "Yes, I know, Daddy dear, I'm an ungrateful woman! I suppose your turn will come next, Mark, and then I don't know what I will do!"

CHAPTER IV

Margaret's turn did not come for nearly a year. Then, in Germany again, and lingering at a great Berlin hotel because the spring was so beautiful and the city so sweet with linden bloom, and especially because there were two Americans at the hotel whose game of bridge it pleased Mr. and Mrs. Carr-Boldt daily to hope they could match; then Margaret transformed within a few hours from a merely pretty, very dignified, perfectly contented secretary, entirely satisfied with what she wore as long as it was suitable and fresh, into a living woman who could scarcely understand the change that had overtaken her.

It all came about very simply. One of the

aforementioned bridge players wondered if
Mrs. Carr-Boldt and her niece—oh, wasn't
it?—her secretary then—would like to hear
a very interesting young American professor lecture this morning?—wondered,
when they were fanning themselves in the
airy lecture-room, if they would care to
meet Professor Tenison?

Margaret looked into a pair of keen,
humorous eyes, answered with her own
smile Professor Tenison's sudden charming
one. Then she listened to him talk, as he
strode about the platform, boyishly shaking
back the hair that fell across his forehead.
After that he walked to the hotel with them
through the perfumed spring air. There was
a plunge from the hot street into the
awninged cool gloom of the hotel, and then
a luncheon, when the happy, steady
murmur from their own table seemed
echoed by the murmurous clink and stir
and laughter all about them, and accented
by the not-too-close music from the band.

Doctor Tenison was thoroughly charming, Margaret thought, instantly set at ease by his unaffected, friendly manner. He was a gentleman, to begin with; distinguished at thirty-two in his chosen work; of an old and honored American family, and the only son of a rich—and eccentric—old doctor whom Mrs. Carr-Boldt chanced to know. Mother wrote in a letter that Father had enjoyed reading Doctor Tenison's series in the New York paper and thought him a promising young man.

He was frankly delighted that providence had brought him in contact with these charming people. And as Mrs. Carr-Boldt took an instant fancy to him, and as he was staying at their own hotel, they saw him after that every day and several times a day. Margaret would come down the great sun-bathed stairway in the morning to find him patiently waiting in a porch chair. There would be time for a chat over their fruit and eggs before Mr. Carr-Boldt came down, all ready for a motor-trip, or Mrs. Carr-Boldt, swathed in cream-colored coat and flying veils, joined them with an approving "Good-morning."

Margaret remembered these breakfasts all her life: the sun-splashed little table in a corner of the great dining room, the rosy fatherly waiter who was so delighted with her German, the busy picturesque traffic in the street just below the wide-open window.

The professor joined them for church on Sunday, and sometimes went with them on their morning drive, to be dropped at the lecture-hall with Margaret and Mrs. Carr-Boldt. The latter was pleased to take the course of lectures very seriously, and carried a handsome Russian leather notebook and a gold pencil. Sometimes after luncheon, they all went on an expedition together to explore the city. They would end the afternoon with coffee and little cakes in some tearoom and come home tired and merry in the long shadows of the Spring sunset.

There was one glorious tramp in the rain, when the professor's great laugh rang out like a boy's for sheer high spirits. That day they all had tea in the deserted charming little parlor of the hotel and drank it while toasting their feet over a glowing fire. After Mrs. Carr-Boldt had excused herself to dress for dinner, John Tenison asked, "Is Mrs. Carr-Boldt your mother's or your father's sister?"

"Oh, goodness gracious!" said Margaret, laughing over her teacup. "Haven't I told you yet that I'm only her secretary? I never saw Mrs. Carr-Boldt until five years ago!"

"Perhaps you did tell me. But I got it into my head, that first day, that you were aunt and niece—"

"People do, I think," Margaret said thoughtfully, "because we're both fair." She did not say that but for Mrs. Carr-Boldt's invaluable maid the likeness would have been less marked, on this score at least. "I taught school," she went on simply, "and

Mrs. Carr-Boldt happened to come to my school, and she asked me to come to her."

"You're all alone in the world, Miss Paget?" the direct question came quite naturally.

"Oh, dear me, no! My father and mother are living," and feeling, as she always did, a little claim on her loyalty, she added, "We are, or were, rather, Southern people, but my father settled in a very small New York town."

"Mrs. Carr-Boldt told me that. I'd forgotten," said Professor Tenison, and he carried the matter entirely out of Margaret's hands by continuing, "She tells me that Quincyport was named for your mother's grandfather, and that Judge Paget was your father's father."

"Father's uncle," Margaret corrected, although as a matter of fact Judge Paget had been no nearer than her father's second cousin. "But Father always called him uncle," Margaret assured herself inwardly. To the Quincyport claim she said nothing. Quincyport was in the country that Mother's people had come from. Quincy was a very unusual name, and the original Quincy had been a Charles, which was certainly one of Mother's family names. Margaret and Julie, browsing about among the colonial histories and genealogies of the Weston Public Library years before, had come to a jubilant certainty that Mother's grandfather must have been the same man. But she did not feel quite so positive now.

"Your people are still in the South, you said?"

"Oh, no!" Margaret cleared her throat. "They're in Weston—Weston, New York."

"Weston! Not near Dayton?"

"Why, yes! Do you know Dayton?"

"Do I know Dayton?" He was like an eager child. "Why, my Aunt Pamela lives there; the only mother I ever knew! I knew Weston, too, a little. Lovely homes there, some of them old colonial houses. And your mother lives there? Is she fond of flowers?"

"She loves them," Margaret said, vaguely uncomfortable.

"Well, she must know Aunt Pamela," said John Tenison, enthusiastically. "I expect they'd be great friends. And you must know Aunt Pam. She's like a dainty old piece of china, or a—I don't know, a tea rose! She was never married, and she lives in the most charming brick house with hollyhocks all about it and such an atmosphere inside! She has an old maid and an old gardener, and, don't you know, she's the sort of woman who likes to sit down under a portrait of your great-grandfather, in a dim parlor full of mahogany and rose jars, with her black silk skirts spreading about her, and an Old Blue cup in her hand, and talk family—how cousin this married a man whose people aren't anybody, and cousin that is outraging precedent by naming her child for her husband's side of the house. She's a funny, dear old lady! You, know, Miss Paget," the professor went on, with his eager, familiar manner, "when I met you, I thought you didn't quite seem like a New Yorker. Aunt Pam—you know she's my only mother; I got all my early knowledge from her—Aunt Pam detests the usual New York girl, and the minute I met you I knew she'd like you. You'd sort of fit into the Dayton picture, with your braids and those ruffly things you wear!"

Margaret said simply, "I would love to meet her," and began slowly to pull on her gloves. It surely was not requisite that she should add, "But you must not confuse my home with any such exquisitely ordered existence as that. We are simple people, and our days are filled with simple hard work. We have good blood in our veins, but not more than hundreds of thousands of other American families. My mother would not appreciate one-tenth of your aunt's conversation; your aunt would find very uninteresting the things that are vital to my mother."

No, she couldn't say that. She picked up her dashing little hat and her storm coat and excused herself to prepare for dinner. No, the professor might call on her at Bar Harbor, take a yachting trip with the Carr-Boldts perhaps, and then, when they were good friends, some day she would ask Mother to have a simple little luncheon, and Mrs. Carr-Boldt would let her bring Doctor Tenison down in the motor from New York. Margaret's cheeks burned as her conscience smote her for this obvious disloyalty to her family, but she lifted her chin and tried to shake the feeling off. After all, it wasn't that she was ashamed of her family; she only wanted them to appear at their best when they met her friends.

For two happy weeks, life seemed to grow warmer and more rosy-colored for Margaret. Little things took on a new significance; every moment carried its

freight of joy. There was a new glow in her
cheeks, new lights in the dark-lashed eyes
that were so charming a contrast to her
bright hair.

Then abruptly it ended. Victoria, brought
down from school in Switzerland with
various indications of something wrong,
was in a flash a sick child; a child who must
be hurried home to the only surgeon in
whom the Carr-Boldts placed the least
trust. There was hurried packing, telephon-
ing, wiring; it was only a few hours after the
great German physician's diagnosis that
they were all at the railway station, breathless, nervous, eager to get started.

Doctor Tenison accompanied them to the
station. Arriving as they were departing
were the St. George Allens, noisy, rich,
arrogant New Yorkers, for whom Margaret
had a special dislike. The Allens fell
joyously upon the Carr-Boldt party, with a
confusion of greetings. "And Jack Tenison!"
shouted Lily Allen, delightedly. "Well, what

fun! What are you doing here?"

"I'm feeling a little lonely," said the professor, smiling at Margaret.

"Nothing like that; unsay them woyds," said Maude Allen, cheerfully. "Mamma, make him dine with us! Say you will!"

"I assure you that I was dreading the lonely evening," John Tenison said gratefully. Margaret felt a secret disappointment that she carried through the worried fortnight of Victoria's illness and the busy days that followed; for Mrs. Carr-Boldt had one of many nervous breakdowns, and took her turn at the hospital when Victoria came home. For the first time in five happy years Margaret drooped, and for the first time a longing for money and power of her own gnawed at the girl's heart. She was only a secretary, she told herself bitterly, one of the hundred paid dependents of a rich woman. She was only, after all, a little country school teacher.

CHAPTER V

"So you're going home to your own people for the weekend, Peggy? And how many of you are there, I always forget?" said young Mrs. George Crawford, negligently. She tipped back in her chair, half shut her novel, half shut her eyes, and looked critically at her fingernails.

Outside the big country house summer sunshine flooded the smooth lawns, sparkled on the falling diamonds and still pool of the fountain, glowed over acres of matchless wood and garden. But deep awnings made a clear cool shade indoors, and the wide rooms were delightfully breezy.

Margaret, busy with a ledger and

chequebook, smiled absently, finished a long column, made an orderly entry, and wiped her pen.

"Seven," said she, smiling.

"Seven!" echoed Mrs. Potter, lazily. "My heaven—seven children! How early Victorian!"

"Isn't it?" said a third woman, a very beautiful woman, Mrs. Watts Watson, who was also idling and reading in the white-and-gray morning room. "Well," she added, dropping her magazine and locking her hands about her head, "my grandmother had ten. Fancy trying to raise ten children!"

"Oh, everything's different now," the first speaker said indifferently. "Everything's more expensive; life is more complicated. People used to have roomier houses, aunts and cousins and grandmothers living with them; there was always someone at home with the children. Nowadays we don't do that."

"And thank heaven we don't!" said Mrs.

Watson, piously. "If there's one thing I can't stand, it's a houseful of things-in-law!"

"Of course; but I mean it made the family problem simpler," Mrs. Crawford pursued. "Oh, I don't know! Everything was so simple. All this business of sterilizing and fumigating and pasteurizing and vaccinating and boiling in boracic acid wasn't done in those days," she finished vaguely.

"Now there you are—now there you are!" said Mrs. Carr-Boldt, entering into the conversation with sudden force. Entirely recovered after her nervous collapse, as brisk as ever in her crisp linen gown, she was signing the cheques that Margaret handed her, frowningly busy and absorbed with her accounts. Now she leaned back in her chair, glanced at the watch at her wrist and relaxed the cramped muscles of her body. "That's exactly it, Rose," said she to Mrs. Crawford. "Life is more complicated. People, the very people who ought to have children, simply cannot afford it! And who's

to blame? Can you blame a woman whose
life is packed full of other things she simply
cannot avoid, if she declines to complicate
things any further? Our grandmothers
didn't have telephones or motor-cars or
weekend parties, or even, for that matter,
manicures and hair-dressers! A good heavy
silk was full dress all the year 'round. They
washed their own hair. The 'upstairs girl'
answered the doorbell—why, they didn't
even have talcum powder and nursery
refrigerators and sanitary rugs that have
to be washed every day! Do you suppose my
grandmother ever took a baby's tempera-
ture, or had its eyes and nose examined, or
its adenoids cut? They had more children,
and they lost more children, without any
reason or logic whatever. Poor things, they
never thought of doing anything else, I
suppose! A fat, old nurse brought up the
whole crowd—it makes one shudder to
think of it! Why, I always had a trained
nurse, and the regular nurse used to take

two baths a day. I insisted on that, and both nurseries were washed out every day with chloride of potash solution, and the iron beds were washed every week! And even then Vic had this mastoid trouble, and Harriet got everything, almost."

"Exactly," said Mrs. Watson. "That's you, Hattie, with all the money in the world. Now do you wonder that some of the rest of us, who have to think of money—in short," she finished decidedly, "do you wonder that people are not having children? At first, naturally, one doesn't want them—for three or four years, I'm sure, the thought doesn't come into one's head. But then, afterward— you see, I've been married fifteen years now!—afterward, I think it would be awfully nice to have one or two little kiddies, if it was a possible thing. But it isn't."

"No, it isn't," Mrs. Crawford agreed. "You don't want to have them unless you're able to do everything in the world for them. If I were Hat here, I'd have a dozen."

"Oh, no you wouldn't," Mrs. Carr-Boldt assured her promptly. "No, you wouldn't! You can't leave everything to servants— there are clothes to think of, and dentists, and special teachers, and it's frightfully hard to get a nursery governess. And then you've got to see that they know the right people—don't you know?—and give them parties. I tell you, it's a strain."

"Well, I don't believe my mother with her seven ever worked any harder than you do!" said Margaret, with the admiration in her eyes that was so sweet to the older woman. "Look at this morning—did you sit down before you came in here twenty minutes ago?"

"I? Indeed I didn't!" Mrs. Carr-Boldt said. "I had my breakfast and letters at seven, bath at eight, straightened out that squabble between Swann and the cook—I think Paul is still simmering, but that's neither here nor there!—then I went down with the vet to see the mare. Joe'll never

forgive me if I've really broken the crea-
ture's knees! Then I telephoned mother
and saw Harriet's violin man and talked to
that Italian Joe sent up to clean the oil
paintings—he's in the gallery now, and—
let's see—"

"Italian lesson," prompted Margaret.

"Italian lesson," the other echoed, "and
then came in here to sign my cheques."

"You're so executive, Harriet," said Mrs.
Crawford, languidly.

"Apropos of Swann," Margaret said, "he
confided to me that he has seven children—on a little farm in Long Island."

"The butler—oh, I dare say!" Mrs. Watson
agreed. "They can, because they've no stan-
dard to maintain—seven, or seventeen—
the only difference in expense is the actual
amount of bread and butter consumed."

"It's too bad," said Mrs. Crawford. "But
you've got to handle the question sanely
and reasonably, like any other. Now, I love
children," she went on. "I'm perfectly crazy

about my sister's little girl. She's eleven
now and the cutest thing alive. But when I
think of all Mabel's been through since she
was born, I realize that it's a little too much
to expect of any woman. Now, look at us—
there are thousands of people fixed as we
are. We're in an apartment hotel with one
maid. There's no room for a second maid,
no porch, and no backyard. Well, the baby
comes—one loses, before and after the
event, just about six months of everything,
and of course the expense is frightful, but
no matter!—the baby comes. We take a
house. That means three indoor maids,
George's chauffeur, a man for lawn and
furnace—that's five—"

"Doubling expenses," said Mrs. Carr-
Boldt, thoughtfully.

"Doubling—! Trebling or more. But
that's not all. Baby must be out from eleven
to three every day. So you've got to go sit by
the carriage in the park while nurse goes
home for her lunch. Or, if you're out for

luncheon, or giving a luncheon, she brings baby home, bumps the carriage into the basement, carries the baby upstairs, eats her lunch in snatches—the maids don't like it, and I don't blame them! I know how it was with Mabel; she had to give up that wonderful old apartment of theirs on Gramercy Park. Sid had his studio on the top floor, and she had such a lovely flat on the next floor, but there was no lift and no laundry, and the kitchen was small—a baby takes so much fussing! And then she lost that splendid cook of hers, Germaine. She wouldn't stand it. Up to that time she'd been cooking and waiting, too, but the baby ended that. Mabel took a house, and Sid paid studio rent besides, and they had two maids, and then three maids—and what with their fighting, and their days off, and eternally changing, Mabel was a wreck. I've seen her trying to play a bridge hand with Dorothy bobbing about on her arm— poor girl! Finally, they went to a hotel, and of course the child got older and was less trouble. But to this day Mabel doesn't dare leave her alone for one second. And when they go out to dinner, and leave her with the maid in the hotel, of course the child cries—!"

"That's the worst of a kiddie," Mrs. Watson said. "You can't ever turn 'em off, as it were, or make it spades! They're always right on the job. I'll never forget Elsie Clay. She was the best friend I had, and my bridesmaid, too. She married, and after a while they took a house in Jersey because of the baby. I went out there to lunch one day. There she was in a house perfectly buried in trees, with the rain sopping down outside and smoke blowing out of the fireplace and the drawing room as dark as pitch at two o'clock. Elsie said she used to nearly die of loneliness, sitting there all afternoon long listening to the trains whistling and the maid thumping irons in the kitchen and picking up the baby's blocks. And they quarreled, you know, she and her husband—that was the beginning of the trouble. Finally the boy went to his grandmother, and now I believe Elsie's married again and living in California somewhere."

Margaret, hanging over the back of her chair, was an attentive listener.

"But people—people in town have children!" she said. "The Blankenships have one, and haven't the de Normandys?"

"The Blankenship boy is in college," said Mrs. Carr-Boldt, "and the little de Normandys lived with their grandmother until they were old enough for boarding school."

"Well, the Deans have three!" Margaret said triumphantly.

"Ah well, my dear! Harry Dean's a rich man, and she was a Pell of Philadelphia," Mrs. Crawford supplied promptly. "Now the Eastmans have three, too, with a trained nurse apiece."

"I see," Margaret admitted slowly.

"Far wiser to have none at all," said Mrs. Carr-Boldt in her decisive way, "than to handicap them from the start by letting them see other children enjoying pleasures and advantages they can't afford. And now, girls, let's stop wasting time. It's half-past eleven. Why can't we have a game of auction right here and now?"

Margaret returned to her chequebook with speed. The other two, glad to be aroused, heartily approved the idea.

"Well, what does this very busi-nesslike aspect imply?" Mrs. Carr-Boldt asked her secretary.

"It means that I can't play cards, and you oughtn't," Margaret said, laughing.

"Oh? Why not?"

"Because you've lots of things to do, and I've got to finish these notes, and I have to sit with Harriet while she does her German."

"Where's Fräulein?"

"Fräulein's going to drive Vic over to the

Partridges' for luncheon, and I promised
Swann I'd talk to him about favors and
things for tomorrow night."

"Well—busy Lizzie! And what have I to do?"

Margaret reached for a well-filled date-
book. "You were to decide about those alter-
ations, the porch and dining room, you
know," said she. "There are some architect's
sketches around here; the man's going to
be here early in the morning. You said
you'd drive to the yacht club to see about
the stage for the children's play; you were
to stop on the way back and see old Mrs.
McNab a moment. You wanted to write
Mrs. Polk a note to catch the Kaiserin
Augusta, and luncheon's early because of
the Kellogg bridge." She shut the book.
"And call Mr. Carr-Boldt at the club at
one," she added.

"All that, now fancy!" said her employer,
admiringly. She had swept some scattered
magazines from a small table and was now
seated there, negligently shuffling a pack

of cards in her fine white hands.

"Ring, will you, Peggy?" she asked.

"And the boat races are today, and you dine at Oaks-in-the-Field," Margaret supplemented inflexibly.

"Yes? Well, come and beat the seven of clubs," said Mrs. Carr-Boldt, spreading the deck for a draw.

"Fräulein," she said sweetly a moment later when a maid had summoned that worthy and earnest governess, "tell Miss Harriet that Mother doesn't want her to do her German today; it's too warm. Tell her that she's to go with you and Miss Victoria for a drive. Thank you. And, Fräulein, will you telephone old Mrs. McNab and say that Mrs. Carr-Boldt is lying down with a severe headache, and she won't be able to come in this morning? Thank you. And, Fräulein, telephone the yacht club, will you? And tell Mr. Mathews that Mrs. Carr-Boldt is indisposed and he'll have to come back this afternoon. I'll talk to him before the children's races. And, one thing more! Will you tell Swann Miss Paget will see him about tomorrow's dinner when she comes back from the yacht club today? And tell him to send us something cool to drink now. Thank you so much. No, shut it. Thank you. Have a nice drive!"

They all drew up their chairs to the table.

"You and I, Rose," said Mrs. Watson. "I'm so glad you suggested this, Hattie. I am dying to play."

"It really rests me more than anything else," said Mrs. Carr-Boldt. "Two spades."

CHAPTER VI

Archerton, a blur of flying trees and houses, bright in the late sunlight; Pottsville, with children wading and shouting under the bridge; Hunt's Crossing, then the next would be Weston and home.

Margaret, beginning to gather wraps and small possessions together, sighed. She sighed partly because her head ached, partly because the hot trip had mussed her usual fresh trimness, largely because she was going home.

This was August; her last trip home had been between Christmas and New Year's. She had sent a box home from Germany at Easter with ties for the boys, silk scarves

for Rebecca, books for Dad. She had
written Mother for her birthday in June
and enclosed an exquisite bit of lace in the
letter, but although Victoria's illness had
brought her to America nearly three
months ago, it had somehow been impossible, she wrote them, to come home until
now. Margaret had paid a great deal for the
lace, as a sort of salve for her conscience—
not that Mother would ever wear it!

Here was Weston. Weston looking pitiful
under the heartless rays of the afternoon
sun. The town, like most of its inhabitants,
was wilted and grimed after the burden
and heat of the long summer day. Margaret
carried her heavy suitcase slowly up Main
Street. Shop windows were spotted and
dusty, and shopkeepers, standing hot and
idle in their doorways, looked spotted and
dusty, too. A cloud of flies fought and
surged about the closely guarded door of
the butcher shop; a delivery cart was at the
curb, the discouraged horse switching an

ineffectual tail.

As Margaret passed this car, a tall boy of fourteen came out of the shop with a bang of the wire-netting door and slid a basket into the back of the car.

"Teddy!" said Margaret, irritation evident in her voice in spite of herself.

"Hello, Mark!" said her brother delightedly. "Say, great to see you! Get in on the four-ten?"

"Ted," said Margaret, kissing him, as the Pagets always quite simply kissed each other when they met, "what are you driving Costello's cart for?"

"Like to," said Theodore simply. "Mother doesn't care. Say, you look swell, Mark!"

"What makes you want to drive this horrid cart, Ted?" protested Margaret. "What does Costello pay you?"

"Pay me?" scowled her brother, taking up the reins. "Oh, come out of it, Marg'ret! He doesn't pay me much of anything. Don't you make Mother stop me, either, will you?" he ended anxiously.

"Of course I won't!" Margaret said impatiently.

"Giddap, Ruth!" said Theodore; but departing, he pulled up to add, "Say, Dad didn't get his raise this year."

"Did?" said Margaret, brightening.

"Didn't!" He grinned affectionately upon her as with a dislocating jerk the cart started a ricocheting career down the street with abandon known only to butcher's carts. Margaret, changing her heavy suitcase to the rested arm, was still vexedly watching it, when two girls, laughing in the open doorway of the express company's office across the street, caught sight of her. One of them, a little vision of pink hat and ruffles and dark eyes and hair, came running to join her.

Rebecca was now sixteen, and of all the handsome Pagets the best to look upon. She was dressed girlishly but with all the skill her mother's needle could command, pink ribbons streaming from her little hat. Rebecca had grown up in eight months, her sister thought, confusedly; she was no longer the adorable, un-self-conscious tomboy who skated and tobogganed with the boys.

"Hello, darling dear!" said Rebecca. "Too bad no one met you! We all thought you were coming in on the six. Crazy about your suit! Here's Maudie Pratt. You know Maudie, don't you Mark?"

Margaret knew Maudie. Rebecca's infatuation for plain, complacent Miss Pratt was a standing mystery in the Paget family. Margaret smiled and bowed.

"I think we stumbled upon a little secret of yours today, Miss Margaret," said Maudie with her best company manner as they walked along. Margaret raised her eyebrows. "Rebby and I," Maudie went on—Rebecca was at the age that seeks a piquant substitute for an unpoetical name—"Rebby and I are wondering if we may ask you who Mr. John Tenison is?"

John Tenison! Margaret's heart stood still with a shock almost sickening, then went on beating at a rapid pace. Coloring high, she looked sharply at Rebecca.

"Cheer up, angel," said Rebecca, "he's not dead. He sent a telegram today, and Mother opened it—"

"Naturally," said Margaret, concealing an agony of impatience, as Rebecca paused apologetically.

"He's with his aunt, at Dayton, up the road here," continued Rebecca, "and wants you to wire him if he may come down and spend tomorrow here."

Margaret drew a relieved breath. There was time to turn around, at least.

"Who is he, sis?" asked Rebecca.

"Why, he's an awfully clever professor, dear," Margaret answered serenely. "We heard him lecture in Germany this spring and met him afterward. I liked him very much. He's tremendously interesting." She tried to keep her voice calm and even. "Father has read his work," she added, "and he believes he is a most promising man."

He wanted to come to see her. He must have telephoned and asked to call, or he would not have known that she was at home this weekend. What did it mean? Surely it was significant. The thought was all joy. But, on the other hand, there was instantly the miserable conviction that he mustn't be allowed to come to Weston, no—no—she couldn't have him see her home and her family on a crowded hot summer Sunday, when the town looked its dreariest and the children were home from school, and when the scramble to get to church and to safely accomplish the one o'clock dinner exhausted the women of the family. How could she keep him from coming; what excuse could she give?

"Don't you want him to come—is he old and fussy?" asked Rebecca, interestedly.

"I'll see," Margaret answered vaguely.

"No, he's only thirty-two or four."

"And charming!" said Maudie archly. Margaret eyed her with a coolness worthy of Mrs. Carr-Boldt herself, then turned rather pointedly to Rebecca.

"How's Mother, Becky?"

"Oh, she's fine!" Rebecca said absently, in her turn.

Margaret looked sideways at Rebecca—the dainty little figure, the even ripple and curl of her plaited hair, the assured pose of the pretty head. Victoria Carr-Boldt, just Rebecca's age, was a big schoolgirl still, self-conscious and inarticulate, her well-groomed hair in an unbecoming "club," her well-hung skirts unbecomingly short. Margaret had half expected to come home and find Rebecca at the same stage of development.

Rebecca cheerfully observed, "Dad didn't get his raise this year—isn't that the limit?"

Margaret sighed again, shrugged wearily. They were in their own quiet side street now, a street lined with shabby little houses and beautified by magnificent old elms and maples. The Pagets' own particular gate was weather-peeled, the lawn trampled and bare. A bulging wire-netting door gave on the shabby old hall Margaret knew so well. She went on into the familiar rooms, acutely conscious, as she always was for the first hour or two at home, of the bareness everywhere—the old sofa that sagged in the seat, the scratched rockers, the bookcases overflowing with coverless magazines, and the old square piano half-buried under loose sheets of music.

Duncan sat on the piano bench, gloomily sawing at a violoncello. Robert, nine now, with all his pretty baby roundness gone and big teeth missing when he smiled, stood in the bay window, twisting the already limp net curtains into a tight rope. Each boy gave Margaret a kiss that seemed curiously to taste of dust, sunburn, and freckles, before she followed the noise of hissing and voices to the kitchen to find Mother.

The kitchen, at five o'clock on Saturday afternoon, was in wild confusion and insufferably hot. Margaret had a distinct impression that not a movable article therein was in place, and not an available inch of tables or chairs unused, before her eyes reached the tall figure of the woman in a gown of chocolate percale, who was frying cutlets at the big range. Her face was dark with heat and streaked with perspiration. She turned as Margaret entered and gave a delighted cry.

"Well, there's my girl! Bless her heart! Look out for this spoon, lovey," she added immediately, giving the girl a guarded embrace. Tears of joy stood frankly in her fine eyes.

"I meant to have all this out of the way, dear," apologized Mrs. Paget, with a gesture that included cakes in the process of frosting, salad vegetables in the process of cooling, soup in the process of getting strained, great loaves of bread that sent a delicious fragrance over all the other odors. "But we didn't look for you until six."

"Oh, no matter!" Margaret said bravely.

"Did Rebecca tell you Dad didn't get his raise?" called Mrs. Paget, in a voice that rose above the various noises of the kitchen. "Blanche!" she protested, "can't that wait?" for the old servant had begun to crack ice with deafening smashes. But Blanche did not hear, so Mrs. Paget continued loudly, "Dad saw Redman himself; he'll tell you about it. Don't stay in the kitchen in that pretty dress, dear! I'm coming right upstairs."

It was very hot upstairs; the bedrooms smelled faintly of matting, the soap in the bathroom was shriveled in its saucer. In Margaret's old room the week's washing had been piled high on the bed. She took off her hat and linen coat, brushed her hair back from her face, flinging her head back and shutting her eyes the better to fight tears as she did so, and began to sort the collars and shirts and put them away.

Her last journey took her to the big third-story room where the three younger boys slept. The western sunlight poured over beds that Mother had carefully made and over the scattered small possessions that seem to ooze from the pores of little boys. Margaret set her lips distastefully as she brought order out of chaos. It was all wrong, somehow, she thought, gathering handkerchiefs and matches and the oiled paper that had wrapped caramels.

She went out on the porch in time to put her arms about her father's shoulders when he came in. Mr. Paget told his wife and daughters that he thought he might be coming down with something. Margaret's mother met this statement with an anxious solicitude that was very soothing to the sufferer. She made Mark get Daddy his slippers and loose coat and suggested that Rebecca shake up the dining room couch before she established him there in a rampart of pillows.

Mr. Paget, reclining, shut his eyes, remarked that it had been a rough day, and wondered if "somebody" would be kind enough to make him just a little milk toast for his dinner. He smiled at Margaret when she sat down beside him; all the children were dear, but the oldest daughter knew she held a special place with her father.

"I must be getting to be an old man!" he said with a slight laugh, and Margaret responded in a soothing tone, "Don't talk that way, Father, darling!" She listened to a long account of the "raise," holding her father's hand and shaking her head at the unfairness of it all. Dad was at least the equal of anyone in Weston! Why, a man Dad's age shouldn't have to ask for a raise—he ought to be dictating by now. It was all wrong.

"Dinner!" bellowed the nine-year-old

Robert, breaking into the room at this point, and "Dinner!" said Mrs. Paget cheerfully from the chair into which she had dropped at the table. Mr. Paget, revived by sympathy, milk toast, and his daughters' kind attentions, took his place at the head, and Bruce the chair between Margaret and his mother. Like the younger boys, whose almost confluent freckles had been brought into unusual prominence by violently applied soap and water, and whose hair dripped on their collars, he had brushed up for dinner, but his shirt and corduroy trousers were stained and spotted from machine oil. Margaret, comparing him secretly to the men she knew, as daintily groomed as women, in their spotless white, felt a little resentment that Bruce's tired face was so contented and said to herself again that it was all wrong.

Dinner was the same meal with which she was so familiar: Blanche supplying an occasional reproof to the boys; Ted having to be reminded to eat his vegetables and ready in an incredibly short time for a second cutlet; and Robert begging for corn syrup, then spilling it from his bread. Mrs. Paget disappeared kitchenward frequently. She wanted Margaret to tell her all about Mr. Tenison. Margaret laughed and assured her there was nothing new to tell.

"You might get a horse and buggy from Peterson's," suggested Mrs. Paget interestedly, "and drive about after dinner."

"Oh, Mother, I don't think I had better let him come!" Margaret said. "There's so many of us and such confusion on Sunday! Ju and Harry are almost sure to come over."

"Yes, I guess they will," Mrs. Paget said, with her sudden radiant smile. "Ju is so dear in her little house, and Harry's so sweet with her," she went on with vivacity. "Father and I had dinner with them Tuesday. Bruce said Rebecca was lovely with the boys—we're going to Julie's again soon. I declare, it's so long since we'd been anywhere without the children that we both felt funny. It was a lovely evening."

"You're too much tied, Mother," Margaret said affectionately.

"Not now!" her mother protested radiantly. "With all my babies turning into men and women so fast. And I'll have you all together tomorrow, and your friend I hope, too, Mark," she added hospitably. "You had better let him come, dear. There's a big dinner, and I always freeze more cream than we need, anyway, because Father likes a plate of it about four o'clock."

"Well, but there's nothing to do," Margaret protested.

"No, but dinner takes quite a while," Mrs. Paget suggested a little doubtfully, "and we could have a nice talk on the porch, and then you could go driving or walking. I wish there was something cool and pleasant to do, Mark," she finished a little wistfully. "You just do as you wish about asking him to come."

"I think I'll wire him that another time would be better," said Margaret, slowly.

Mother looked quickly at Father, who returned her glance knowingly. He placed his hand on Margaret's. "Some other time we'll send the boys off before dinner and have things all nice and quiet, Margaret," he said. "How would that be?"

Mother nodded in agreement. Margaret looked at her as if she found something new in the bright face. She could not understand why her mother, still too heated to commence eating her dinner, should radiate such contentment, as she sat back, a little breathless after the flurry of serving. She herself felt injured and sore, not at the mere disappointment of John Tenison's visit, but because she felt more acutely than ever tonight the difference between his world and her own.

"Something nice has happened, Mother?" she hazarded, entering with an effort into the older woman's mood.

"Nothing special." Her mother's happy eyes ranged about the circle of young faces. "But it's so lovely to have you here, and to have Ju coming tomorrow," she said. "I just wish Daddy could build a house for each one of you, as you marry and settle down, right around our house in a circle, as they say people do sometimes in the Old World. I think then I'd have nothing in life to wish for!"

"Oh, Mother—in Weston!" Margaret said hopelessly, but her mother did not catch it.

"Not, Mark," she went on hastily and earnestly, "that I'm not more than grateful to God for all His goodness, as it is! I look at other women, and I wonder, I wonder— what I have done to be so blessed! Mark—" her face suddenly glowed, she leaned a little toward her daughter, "dearie, I must tell you," she said, "it's about Ju—"

Their eyes met in the pause.

"Mother, really?" Margaret said slowly.

"She told me on Tuesday," Mrs. Paget

said, with glistening eyes. "Now, not a word to anyone, Mark, but she'll want you to know!"

"And is she glad?" Margaret said, hesitant to rejoice.

"Glad?" Mrs. Paget echoed, her face gladness itself.

"Well, Ju's so young—just twenty-one," Margaret submitted a little uncertainly, "and she's only just married and in the new house! And I thought they were going to Europe!"

"Oh, Europe!" Mrs. Paget dismissed it cheerfully. "Why, it's the happiest time in a woman's life, Mark! Or I don't know, though," she went on thoughtfully, "I don't know but what I was happiest when you were all tiny, tumbling about me and climbing into my lap. . . . Why, you love children, dear," she finished with a shade of reproach in her voice, as Margaret still looked sober.

"Yes, I know, Mother," Margaret said.

"But Julie's only got the one maid, and I don't suppose they can have another. I hope to goodness Ju won't get herself all run down!"

Her mother laughed. "You remind me of Grandma Paget," said she, smiling. "She lived ten miles away when we were married, but she came in when Bruce was born. She was a rather proud, cold woman herself, but she was very sweet to me. Well, then little Charlie came, fourteen months later, and she took that very seriously. Mother was dead, you know, and Grandma stayed with me again and worried me half sick telling me that it wasn't fair to Bruce and Charlie to divide my time between them that way. Well, then when my third baby was coming, I didn't dare tell her! Finally, she went to visit Aunt Rebecca out west, and it was the very day she got back that the baby came. She came upstairs— she'd come right up from the train and hadn't seen anyone but Dad; and he wasn't very intelligible in his excitement, I guess—and she sat down and took the baby in her arms, and says she, looking at me sort of patiently, yet as if she was exasperated, too: 'Well, this is a nice way to do, the minute my back's turned! What are you going to call her, Julia?' And I said, 'I'm going to call her Margaret, for my dear husband's mother, and she's going to be beautiful and good and grow up to marry the president!'" Mrs. Paget's merry laugh rang out. "I never shall forget your grandmother's face. Just the same," Mrs. Paget added, with a sudden deep sigh, "when little Charlie left us the next year, and Brucie and Dad were both so ill, she and I agreed that you—you were just talking and trying to walk—were the best comfort we had! I could wish my girls no greater happiness than my children have been to me," finished Mother, contentedly.

"I know," Margaret began, half angrily, "but what about the children?" she was going to add. But somehow the arguments she had heard used so plausibly did not utter themselves easily to Mother, whose children would carry into their own middle age a wholesome dread of her displeasure. Margaret faltered and merely scowled.

"I don't like to see that expression on your face, dearie," her mother said, as she might have said it to an eight-year-old child. "Be my sweet girl! Why, marriage isn't marriage without children, Mark. I've been thinking all week of having a baby in my arms again—it's been so long since Bob was a baby."

Margaret devoted herself, with a rather sullen face, to her dessert. Mother would never feel as she did about these things, and what was the use of arguing?

Changing her dress later in a room that was insufferably hot, Margaret reflected that another forty-eight hours would see her speeding back to the world of cool, awninged interiors, uniformed maids, the clink of iced glasses, the flash of white sails on blue water. She could surely afford for that time to be patient and sweet. She lifted Rebecca's starched petticoat from the bed to give Mother a seat, when Mother came in to watch them.

"Sweet girl to take the children to the concert, Mark," said Mother, appreciatively. "I was going to ask Brucie, but he's gone to bed, poor fellow. He's worn out tonight."

"He had a letter from Ned Gunther this morning," said Rebecca cheerfully, "and I think it made him blue all day."

"Ned Gunther?" queried Margaret.

"Chum from college," Rebecca elucidated, "a lot of them are going to Honolulu, just for this month, and of course they wanted Bruce."

Margaret's heart ached for the beloved brother's disappointment. There it was again—all wrong! Before she left the house with the rioting youngsters, she ran upstairs to his room. Bruce, surrounded by scientific magazines, a drop-light with a vivid green shade over his shoulder, looked up with a welcoming smile.

"Sit down and talk, Mark," he said. Margaret explained her hurry.

"Bruce, this isn't much fun!" she said, looking about the room with its shabby dresser and worn carpet. "Why aren't you going to the concert?"

"Is there a concert?" he asked, surprised.

"Why, didn't you hear us talking at dinner?"

"Well—sure! I meant to go to that. I forgot it was tonight," he said with his lazy smile. "I came home and forgot everything."

"Oh, come!" Margaret urged, as eagerly as Rebecca ever did. "It's early, Bruce, come on! You don't need to shave! We'll hold a seat—come on!"

"Sure, I will!" he said, suddenly roused. The magazines rapped on the floor, and Margaret had barely shut the door behind her when she heard his bare feet follow them.

It was like old times to sit next to him through the merry evening, while Rebecca glowed like a little rose among her friends. Margaret had sent a telegram to Professor Tenison, and felt relieved that at least that strain was spared her.

Afterward they strolled back slowly through the inky summer dark, finding the house hot and close when they came in. Margaret went upstairs, hearing her mother's apologetic, "Oh, Father, why didn't I give you back your club?" as she passed the dining room door. She knew Mother didn't care for playing whist and wondered rather irritably why she played it. The Paget family was slow to settle down. Robert became tearful before he was finally bumped protesting into bed. Theodore and Duncan prolonged their ablutions until the noise of shouting, splashing, and thumping in the bathroom brought Mother to the foot of the stairs. Rebecca was conversational. She lay with her slender arms locked behind her head on the pillow and talked, as Julie had talked on that memorable night five years ago. Margaret, restless in the hot darkness, wondering whether the maddening little shaft of light from the hall gas was annoying enough to warrant the effort of getting up and extinguishing it, listened and listened to Rebecca's girlish chatter.

Awakened from uneasy drowsing with a start, Margaret turned over in bed. The hall was dark now, the room cooler. Rebecca was asleep. Hands, hands she knew well, were drawing a light covering over her shoulders. She opened her eyes to see her mother.

"I've been wondering if you're disappointed about Mr. Tenison not coming tomorrow, Mark?" said the tender voice. "For you know we'd love to have him come."

"Oh, no-o!" said Margaret heartily. "Mother, why are you up so late?"

"Just going to bed," said the other, soothingly. "Blanche forgot to put the oatmeal in the cooker, and I went downstairs again. I'll say my prayers in here."

Margaret went off to sleep again, as she had so many hundred times before, with her mother kneeling beside her.

CHAPTER VII

It seemed but a few moments before the blazing Sunday was precipitated upon them, and everybody was late for everything.

The kitchen was filled with the smoke from hot griddles when Margaret went downstairs; and in the dining room the beamimg sunshine fell mercilessly upon the sticky syrup pitcher and upon the stains on the tablecloth. Cream had been brought in the bottle, the bread tray was heaped with orange skins, and the rolls were piled on the tablecloth. Bruce was dividing his attention between Robert and his watch. Rebecca, daintily busy with her breakfast, was all ready for the day, except as to dress, wearing a kimono over her blue ribbons and starched embroideries. Confusion reigned. The younger boys were urged to hurry. At last Mr. Paget took the youngest boys by the hand and marshaled the girls out the door. Mother followed last, checking to make sure Blanche had put the rolls in the warmer to rise for Sunday dinner.

The walk to church was hot, but it was still hotter walking home in the burning midday stillness. Main Street was deserted. A languid little breeze brought small relief. Father and the boys had left church slightly ahead of the women, since Mother had stayed behind to ask a recipe of Mrs. Hawkins. Rebecca and Margaret escorted her home.

"Who's that on the porch?" asked Rebecca, suddenly, as they neared home, spotting a stranger among her father and the boys. Margaret, glancing up sharply, saw, almost with a sensation of sickness, the big, manly figure, the beaming smile, and the shock of dark hair that belonged to John Tenison. She could feel her heartbeat as she went up the steps and gave him her hand.

Oh, if he only couldn't stay to dinner, she prayed. Oh, if only he could spare them time for no more than a flying visit! She forced a smile.

"Doctor Tenison, this is very nice of you!" Margaret said. "Have you met my father— my small brothers?"

"We have been having a great talk," said John Tenison genially, "and this young man," he indicated Robert, "has been showing me the colored supplement of the paper. I didn't have any word from you, Miss Paget," he went on, "so I took the chance of finding you home. And your mother has assured me that I will not put her out by staying to have luncheon with you."

Margaret looked quickly at Mother,

wondering when she had had the time to give Doctor Tenison that information. "Oh, that's nice!" she said mechanically, trying to dislodge Robert from the most comfortable chair by a significant touch of her fingers on his small shoulder. When he was finally dislodged, she sat down, still flushed from her walk and the nervousness Doctor Tenison's arrival caused her, and tried to bring the conversation into a normal channel. But an interruption occurred in the arrival of Harry and Julie in the runabout; the little boys swarmed down to examine it. Julie, very pretty, with a perceptible little new air of dignity, went upstairs to freshen hair and gown, and Harry, pushing his straw hat back the better to mop his forehead, immediately engaged Doctor Tenison's attention with the details of a particularly complicated operation.

Feeling awkward and unsettled, Margaret slipped away and went into the kitchen to distract herself with the dinner preparations. The room presented a scene if possible a little more confused than that of the day before, and it was certainly hotter. Her mother hurried about in a fresh gingham dress. Blanche, moaning "The Palms" with the insistence of one who wishes to show her entire familiarity with a melody, was at the range.

Roast veal, a mountain of mashed potatoes, corn on the cob, and an enormous salad mantled with mayonnaise— Margaret could have wept over the hopelessly plebian dinner!

"Mother, mayn't I get down the finger-bowls," she asked, "and mayn't we have black coffee in the silver pot afterward?"

Mrs. Paget looked absently at her for a dubious second. "I don't like to ask Blanche to wash all that extra glass," she said, in an undertone, adding briskely to Theodore, "No, no, Ted! Stay out of the cake!" and to Blanche herself, "Don't leave the door open when you go in, Blanche; I just drove all the flies out of the dining room." Then she returned to Margaret with a cordial, "Why, certainly, dear! Any one who wants coffee, after tea, can have it! Father always wants his cup of tea."

"Nobody but us ever serves tea with dinner!" Margaret muttered, but her mother did not hear it. She straightened her back irritably and pushed down her rolled-up sleeves.

"We're all ready, Mark—go and tell them, dear! All right, Blanche."

Ruffled and out-of-sorts, Margaret went to summon the others to dinner. Maudie had joined them on the porch now and had been urged to stay.

"Well, he'll have to leave on the five o'clock!" Margaret reflected, purposed to endure until that time. But everything went wrong, and dinner was one long nightmare for her. Professor Tenison's napkin turned out to be a traycloth. Blanche asked for another, disappeared for several minutes and returned without it, to whisper in Mrs. Paget's ear. Mrs. Paget immediately sent her own fresh napkin to the guest. The incident, or something in their murmured conversation, gave Rebecca and Maudie "the giggles." There seemed an exhausting amount of passing and repassing of plates. The room was hot, the supply of ice insufficient.

John Tenison behaved charmingly, eating his dinner with enjoyment, looking interestedly from one face to another, sympathetic, alert, and amused. But Margaret writhed in spirit at what he must be thinking.

Finally the ice cream and the chocolate cake made their appearance; and although these were regular Sunday treats, the boys felt called upon to cheer. Julie asked her mother in an audible undertone if she "ought" to eat cake. Doctor Tenison produced an enormous box of chocolates, and Margaret was disgusted with the frantic scramble her brothers made to secure them.

"If you're going for a walk, dear," her mother said, when the meal was over, "you'd better go. It's almost three now."

"I don't know whether we will; it's so hot," Margaret said, in an indifferent tone, but she could easily have broken into disheartened tears.

"Oh, go," Julie urged, "it's much cooler out." They were up in Margaret's old room, Mrs. Paget tying a big apron about Julie's ruffled frock, preparatory to an attack upon the kitchen. "We think he's lovely," the little matron went on approvingly. When Mrs. Paget had gone downstairs, Julie came very simply and charmingly over to her sister, and standing close beside her with embarrassed eyes on her own hand—very youthful in its plain ring—as she played with the bureau furnishing, she said,

"Mother tell you?"

Margaret looked down at the flushed face.

"Are you sorry, Ju?"

"Sorry!" The conscious eyes flashed into view. "Sorry!" Julie echoed in astonishment. "Why, Mark," she said dreamily—there was no affectation of maturity in her manner now, and it was all the more impressive for that. "Why, Mark," said she, "it's—it's the most wonderful thing that ever happened to me! I think and think"—her voice dropped very low—"of holding it in my arms—mine and Harry's, you know—and of its little face!"

Margaret, stirred, kissed the wet lashes.

"Ju, but you're so young—you're such a baby yourself!" she said.

"Oh, Mark," Julie said, unheeding, "I didn't know what I was saying when we talked that last time. I didn't understand."

Margaret looked away, unable to meet the joyful light in Julie's eyes. "And Harry is so happy, dear. What does Europe matter, or anything else, for that matter? And, Mark," Julie continued, "you know what

Harry and I are going to call her, if it's a girl? Not for Mother, for it's so confusing to have two Julias, but for you! Because," her arms went about her sister, "you've always been such a darling to me, Mark!"

Margaret went downstairs very thoughtfully and out into the silent Sunday streets. Her head ached, and she knew that the village looked very commonplace and that the day was very hot. She found it more painful than sweet to be strolling along beside the tall figure and to send an occasional side glance to John Tenison's earnest face, which wore its pleasantest expression now. Ah, well, it would be all over at five o'clock, she said wearily to herself, and she could go home and lie down with her aching head in a darkened room and try not to think what today might have been. Try not to think of the dainty little luncheon Annie would have given them at Mrs. Carr-Boldt's, of the luxurious choice of amusements afterward: motoring over the lovely country roads, rowing on the wide still water, or simply resting in deep chairs on the sweep of velvet lawn above the river.

She came out of a reverie to find Doctor Tenison glancing calmly up from his watch.

"The train was five o'clock, was it?" he asked. "I've missed it!"

"Missed it!" Margaret echoed blankly. Then, as the horrible possibility dawned upon her, "Oh no!"

"Oh, yes—as bad as that!" he said, laughing at her.

Poor Margaret, fighting despair, struggled to recover herself.

"Well, I thought it might have been important to you!" she said, trying to laugh naturally. "There's a seven-six, but it stops everywhere, and a ten-thirty. The ten-thirty is best, because supper's apt to be a little late."

"The ten-thirty," Doctor Tenison echoed contentedly. Margaret's heart sank—five more hours of the struggle! "But perhaps that's an imposition," he said. "Isn't there an inn here where we could have a bite?"

"We aren't in Berlin," Margaret reminded him, almost smiling. "There's a hotel—but Mother would never forgive me for taking any one there! No, we'll take that little walk I told you of, and Mother will give us something to eat later. Perhaps if we're late enough," she added to herself, "we can just have tea and bread and jam after the others."

Suddenly, unreasonably, she felt relaxed and cheerful. The little episode of missing the train had given her the old dear feeling of adventure and comradeship again. Things couldn't be any worse than they had been at noon, anyway. The experience had been thoroughly disenchanting. What did a few hours, more or less, matter? She would let herself enjoy his company.

It was cooler now; the level late shadows were making even Weston pretty. They went up the steep, shady lane to the old graveyard and wandered peacefully, contentedly among the old graves. Margaret gathered her skirts from contact with the tangled, uncut grass; they had to disturb a flock of nibbling sheep to cross to the crumbling wall. Leaning on the uneven stones that formed it, they looked down at the roofs of the village, half lost in treetops, and listened to the barking of dogs and the shrill voices of children. The sun sank lower, lower. There was a feeling of dew in the air as they made their way home.

When, at seven o'clock, they opened the gate, they found on the side porch only Rebecca, enchanting in something pink and dotted, and Mother and Dad.

"Lucky we waited!" said Rebecca, rising and signaling some wordless message to Margaret that required dimples, widened eyes, compressed lips and an expression of utter secrecy. "Supper's all ready," she added casually.

"Where are the others?" Margaret asked,

experiencing the most pleasing sensation she had had in twenty-four hours.

"Ju and Harry went home, Bob's at George's, and the boy's are walking," answered Rebecca, still dimpling mysteriously with additional information. She gave Margaret an eloquent side-glance as she led the way into the dining room. At the doorway, Margaret stopped, astounded.

The room was hardly recognizable now. It was cool and delightful, with the diminished table daintily set for five. The old silver candlesticks and silver teapot presided over blue bowls of berries and the choicest of Mother's preserved fruits. Some one had found time to put fresh parsley about the Canton platter of cold meats, and some one had made a special trip to Mrs. O'Brien's for the cream that filled the Wedgwood pitcher. Margaret felt tears press suddenly against her eyes.

"Oh, Beck!" she could only stammer when the sisters went into the kitchen for hot water and tea biscuits.

"Mother did it," said Rebecca, returning her hug with fervor. "She gave us all an awful talking to after you left! She said here was dear old Mark, who always worked herself to death for us, trying to make a nice impression and to have things go smoothly, and we were all acting like heathens, and everything so confused at dinner, and hot and noisy! So, later, when the boys and I were out walking, we saw you and Doctor Tenison going up toward the graveyard, and I tore home and told Mother he'd missed the five and would be back; it was after five then, and we just flew!

It was all like a pleasant awakening after a troubled dream. As Margaret took her place at the little feast she felt an exquisite refreshing sense of peace and contentment sink into her heart. Mother was so gracious and charming, behind the urn; Rebecca irresistible in her mannerly admiration of the famous professor. Her father was his sweetest self, delightfully reminiscent of his boyhood. But it was to her mother's face that Margaret's eyes returned most often. She wanted—she was vaguely conscious that she wanted—to get away from the voices and laughter and think about Mother. How kind she was, kind and unselfish, and after all, how few people were that in the world! They were clever and witty and rich—plenty of them, but how little kindness there was! How few faces, like her mother's, did not show a line that was not all tenderness and goodness.

They laughed over their teacups like old friends; the professor and Rebecca shouting joyously together, Mr. Paget one broad twinkle, Mrs. Paget radiantly reflecting, as she always did reflect, the others' mood. It was a memorably happy hour.

And after tea they sat on the porch, and the stars came out, and presently the moon sent silver shafts through the dark foliage of the trees. Little Bob came home and climbed silently, contentedly, into his father's lap.

"Sing something, Mark," said Father then, and Margaret, sitting on the steps with her head against her mother's knee, found it very simple to begin in the darkness one of the old hymns he loved:

When peace like a river attendeth my way,
When sorrows like sea billows roll...

Rebecca, sitting on the rail, one slender arm flung above her head about the pillar, joined her own young voice to Margaret's sweet and steady one. "It is well, it is well with my soul." The others hummed a little. John Tenison, sitting watching them, saw in the moonlight a sudden glitter on the mother's cheek.

Presently Bruce came through the splashed silver and black of the street to sit by Margaret, and the younger boys spread themselves comfortably over the lower steps. Before long all their happy voices rose together on "Blessed Be the Tie That Binds" and "Be Still My Soul" and a dozen more of the old songs and hymns that young people have sung for half a century in the summer moonlight.

And then it was time to say good-night to Professor Tenison. "Come again, sir!" said Mr. Paget heartily. "You know you always have a welcome here with us." Doctor Tenison grinned broadly, then turned to shake the boys' extended hands. Rebecca promised to mail him a certain discussed variety of fern the very next day. Bruce's voice sounded all hearty good will as he hoped that he wouldn't miss Doctor Tenison's next visit. Mrs. Paget, her hand in his, raised keen eyes to his face.

"Surely you'll be down our way again?" she asked.

"Oh, surely." The professor was unable to keep his eyes from moving toward Margaret.

"Good-bye for the present, then," she

said with a kind smile.

"Good-bye, Mrs. Paget," said Doctor Tenison. "It has been a great pleasure. I haven't ever had a happier day."

Margaret, used to the extravagant speeches of another world, was stirred by his simple earnestness. Her heart leapt as they walked away together. He liked them—he liked them!

"I know what makes you so different from other women," remarked John Tensison when he and Margaret were further down the street. "It's having that wonderful mother! She—she—well, she's one woman in a million. I don't have to tell you that! It's something to thank God for, a mother like that; it's a privilege to know her. I've been wondering what she gets out of it; but I think I've found it out. This morning, thinking what her life is, I couldn't see what repaid her, do you see?

What made up to her for the unending effort and sacrifice, the pouring out of love and sympathy and help—year after year after year. . ."

He hesitated, but Margaret did not speak.

"You know," he went on musingly, "these days, when women just serenely ignore the question of children, or at most, as a special concession, bring up one or two—just the one or two whose expenses can be comfortably met!—there's something magnificent in a woman like your mother, who begins eight destinies instead of one! She doesn't strain and chafe to express herself through the medium of poetry or music or the stage, but she puts her whole splendid philosophy into her nursery—launches sound little bodies and minds that have their first growth cleanly and purely about her knees. Responsibility—that's what these other women are afraid of! But it seems to me there's no responsibility like that of decreeing that young lives simply shall not be. Why, what good is learning, or elegance of manner, or painfully acquired fitness of speech and taste and point of view, if you are not going to distil it into the growing plants, the only real hope we have in the world? You know, Miss Paget," his smile was very sweet, "there's a higher tribunal than the social tribunal of this world, after all; and it seems to me that a woman who stands there, as your mother will, with a forest of new lives about her, and a record like hers, will—will find she has a Friend at court!" he smiled whimsically. "And you are so like your mother," he added with quiet conviction.

They were at a lonely corner, and a garden fence offering Margaret a convenient support, she laid her arms suddenly upon the rosevine that covered it and her face upon her arms and cried as if her heart would break.

"Why, why—my dear girl!" the professor said, aghast.

"I'm not what you think I am!" Margaret

sobbed out, incoherently. "I'm not different from other women; I'm just as selfish and bad and mean as the worst of them! And I'm not worthy to tie my mother's shoes! Why, I was even ashamed of my family and unwilling to have you introduced to them!"

"Margaret," said John Tenison, giving her shoulders a gentle shake, "I have a confession to make." Margaret glanced up quickly, surprised. "Margaret, this is not the first time I have met your family." He looked keenly into Margaret's tear-wet eyes. She wrinkled her brow and shook her head.

"What do you mean?"

"Darling, I came out here once before while you were still in New York. I wanted to see your father; to talk to him about you!"

The surprise in Margaret's face made John Tenison laugh delightedly. "Why, didn't you suspect, Margaret, dear? Don't you know how I love you? And your father and mother have given me their blessing, if you'll have me!" he finished with an imploring glance.

Margaret's astonishment was complete; her brain reeled with the overwhelming thoughts clambering for her attention. He had seen her family before! And he had still come back! "What a fool I have been," Margaret said, half to herself. Then, looking up at John Tenison, she repeated, "I have been such a fool—such a selfish little girl. I wanted to hide my family from you; I thought you could never truly like me if you saw where I came from."

"But you are who you are because of your family, Margaret! Don't you see that? Haven't you heard what I've been saying? No society woman can hold a candle to a warm, sympathetic, and sacrificing mother such as yours. And what wealthy business-man do you know who can talk as kindly to his wife or children as your father does? When I met your family, I knew beyond a doubt that you were as genuine and warm as I had thought. Margaret?"

Margaret bit her lip to keep it from trembling as she looked into his warm searching eyes. "You know I love you, Margaret, don't you?"

Margaret could not speak. She nodded her head slowly.

"Do you—can you love me, dear?"

After what seemed a long time, Margaret said, with a catch in her voice, "Yes!" Happy tears filled her eyes. John Tenison's face was alight with a joy as he took her hand and placed it firmly within his arm for the rest of the walk to the station.

Coming back from the train half an hour later, Margaret felt as if she walked upon a new earth. The friendly stars seemed just overhead; a thousand delicious odors came from garden beds and recently watered lawns. She moved like one in a dream and was glad to find herself at last lying in the darkness beside the sleeping Rebecca again. Now, now she could think it all through.

It was all so right and wonderful. He

loved her. He had said it. Her own father and mother had blessed his courtship! Margaret pictured herself as his wife. "Doctor and Mrs. John Tenison"—so it would be written. "Doctor Tenison's wife"— "This is Mrs. Tenison"—she seemed already to hear the magical sound of it.

How good God was to send this best of all gifts to her! Ah, the happy years that would date from tonight. "For better or worse," the old words came to her with a new meaning. Poverty, privation, sickness might come—but to bear them with John, to comfort and sustain him, why, that would be the greatest happiness of all! What hardship could be hard that knitted their hearts closer together; what road too steep if they essayed it hand in hand?

And that—her confused thoughts ran on—that was what had changed all life for Julie. She had forgotten Europe, forgotten all the idle ambitions of her girlhood, because she loved her husband; and now the new miracle was to come to her—the miracle of a child, the little perfect promise of the days to come. How marvelous—how marvelous it was! The little, helpless third person, bringing to radiant youth the great final joy to share together. That was life. Julie was living; and although Margaret's own heart was not yet a wife's, and she could not yet find room for the love beyond that, still she was strangely, deeply stirred now by a longing for all the experiences that life held.

In just a few days, she realized with vague wonder, her slowly formed theories had been set at naught; her whole philosophy turned upside down, and, at last, everything seemed right. Had these years of protest and rebellion done no more than lead her in a wide circle, past empty gain and joyless mirth and the dead fruit of riches and idleness, back to her mother's knees again? She had met brilliant women, rich women, courted women—but where among them was one whose face had ever shone as her mother's shone today? The overdressed, idle dowagers; the matrons with their too-gay frocks, their too-full days, their too-rich food; the girls, all crudeness, artifice, all scheming openly for their own advantage—where among them all was happiness? Where among them was one whom Margaret had heard say—as she had heard her mother say so many, many times—"Children, this is a happy day,"— "Thank God for another lovely Sunday all together,"—"Isn't it lovely to get up and find the sun shining?"—"Isn't it delightful to come home hungry to such a nice dinner?"

And what a share of happiness her mother had given the world! How she had planned and worked for them all— Margaret let her arm fall across the sudden ache in her eyes as she thought of the Christmas mornings and the stuffed stockings at the fireplace that proved every childish wish remembered, every little hidden hope guessed! And how her face would beam as she sat at the breakfast table, enjoying her belated coffee, after the cold walk to church, and responding warmly to the onslaught of kisses and hugs that added fresh color to her cold, rosy cheeks! What a mother she was—Margaret remembered her making them all help her clear up the Christmas disorder of tissue paper and ribbons; then came the inevitable bed making, then overshoes and coats for a long walk with Father. They would come back to find the dining room warm, the long table set, the house deliciously fragrant from the immense turkey that their mother, a fresh apron over her holiday gown, was basting at the oven. Then came the feast and games until twilight and more table-setting; and the baby, whoever he was, was tucked away upstairs before tea, and the evening ended with singing, gathered about Mother at the piano.

"How happy we all were!" Margaret

thought; "and how she worked for us!"

And suddenly theories and speculation ended, and she knew. She knew that faithful, self-forgetting service and the love that spends itself over and over, only to be renewed again and again, are the secret to happiness. For another world, perhaps leisure and beauty and luxury—but in this one, "Whosoever loses his life shall gain it." Margaret knew now that her mother was not only the truest, the finest, the most generous woman she had ever known, but the happiest as well.

She thought of other women like her mother; she suddenly saw what made their lives beautiful. She could understand now why Emily Porter, her brave little associate in school-teaching days, was always bright; why Mary Page, plodding home from the long day at the library desk to her little cottage and crippled sister at night, always made one feel the better and happier for meeting her.

Mrs. Carr-Boldt's days were crowded to the last instant, it was true; but what an illusion it was, after all, Margaret said to herself in all honesty, to humor her little fancy that she was a busy woman! Milliner, manicure, butler, chef, club, card table, tea table—these and a thousand things like them filled her day, and they might all be swept away in an hour, and leave no one the worse. Suppose Mrs. Carr-Boldt's own final summons came; there would be a little flurry throughout the great establishment, legal matters to settle, notes of thanks to be written for flowers. Margaret could imagine Victoria and Harriet, awed but otherwise unaffected, home from school in midweek, and to be sent back before the next Monday. Their lives would go on unchanged. Their mother had never buttered bread for them, never searched for their boots and hats, never watched their work and play and called them to her knees for praise and blame. Mr. Carr-Boldt would have his club, his business, his yacht, his motor-cars—he was well accustomed to living in cheerful independence of family claims.

But life without Mother—! In a sick moment of revelation, Margaret saw it. She saw them gathering in the horrible emptiness and silence of the house Mother had kept so warm and bright. She saw her father's stooped shoulders and trembling hands. She saw Julie and Beck, red-eyed, white-cheeked, in fresh black—she seemed to hear the low-toned voices that would break over and over again so cruelly into sobs. What could they do—who could take up the work she laid down—who would watch and plan and work for them all now? Margaret thought of the empty place at the table, of the room that, after all these years, would no longer be "Mother's room—"

Oh, no—no—no! She began to cry softly in the dark. How ungrateful she had been; how ugly and cross and unwilling to help.

God willing, they would hold Mother safe with them for many years. She should live to see some of the fruits of her long labor of love. She should know that with every fresh step in life, with every deepening experience, her children grew to love her better; turned to her more and more! There would come a day—Margaret thrilled to the thought—when little forms would run ahead of John and herself up the worn path, and when their children would be gathered in Mother's experienced arms! Did life hold a more exquisite moment, she wondered, than that in which she would hear her mother praise them?

All her old castles in the air seemed cheap and tinseled tonight beside these tender dreams that had their roots in the real truths of life. Travel and position, gowns and motor-cars, yachts and country houses, these things were to be bought in all their perfection by the highest bidder, and always would be. But love and charac-

ter and service, home and the wonderful
charge of little lives—the "pure religion
breathing household laws" that guided and
perfected the whole—these were not to be
bought; they were only to be prayed for,
worked for, bravely won.

"God has been very merciful to me,"
Margaret said to herself seriously; and in
her old childish fashion she made some
new resolves. If joy came, she would share
it as far as she could; if sorrow, she would
show her mother that her daughter was
not all unworthy of her. Tomorrow, she
thought, she would go to see Julie. Dear old
Ju, whose heart was so full of the little
Margaret! Margaret had a sudden tender
memory of the days when Theodore and
Duncan and Bob were all babies in turn.
Her mother would gather the little daily
supply of fresh clothes from bureau and
chest every morning and carry the little
bathtub into the sunny nursery window
and sit there with only a bobbing downy

head and waving pink fingers visible from the great warm bundle of bath apron . . . . Ju would be doing that now.

And she had sometimes wished, or half formed the wish, that she and Bruce had been the only ones! Yes, came the sudden thought, but it wouldn't have been Bruce and Margaret, after all. It would have been Bruce and Charlie.

With a sickening thud of her heart, Margaret understood. That was what women did, then, when they denied the right of life to the distant, unwanted, possible little person! Calmly, constantly, in all placid philosophy and self-justification, they kept from the world—not only the troublesome new baby, with his tears and his illnesses, his endless claim on mind and body and spirit—but perhaps the glowing beauty of a Rebecca, the buoyant indomitable spirit of a small Robert, whose grip on life, whose energy and ambition were as strong as Margaret's own!

Margaret stirred uneasily and frowned in the dark. It seemed perfectly incredible, it seemed perfectly impossible that if Mother had had only the two—and how many thousands of women didn't have that!—she, Margaret, a pronounced and separate entity, traveled, ambitious, and to become the wife of one of the world's great men, might not have been lying here in the summer night!

All of the fine-sounding theories of Mrs. Carr-Boldt and her friends crumbled to dust. What would they leave when they were gone? All of their high accomplishments and all of the public's applause would die with them. But Margaret could do what Mother did—just take the nearest duty and fulfill it for posterity and eternity, sleep well, and then rise joyfully to fresh effort.

Margaret felt as if she would never sleep again. The summer night was cool, she was cramped and chilly, but still her thoughts raced on, and she could not shut her eyes.

She turned and pressed her face resolutely into the pillow with a great sigh. A moment later there was a gentle rustle at the door.

"Mark," a voice whispered. "Can't you sleep?"

Margaret locked her arms tight about her mother as the older woman knelt beside her. "Why, how cold you are, sweetheart!" her mother protested, tucking covers about her. "I thought I heard you sigh! I got up to lock the stairway door; Bob's gotten a trick of walking in his sleep when he's overtired. It's nearly one o'clock, Mark! What have you been doing?"

"Thinking." Margaret put her lips very close to her mother's ear. "Mother—" she started and then stopped. Mrs. Paget kissed her.

"Father and I knew," she said simply, and further announcement was not needed. "My darling little girl!" she added tenderly; and then, after a silence, "He is very fine, Mark, so unaffected, so gentle and nice with the boys. And Father thinks him a godly man. I'm glad, Mark. I lose my girl, but there's no happiness like a good marriage, my dear."

"No, you won't lose me, Mother," Margaret said, clinging very close. "We hadn't much time to talk, but this much we did decide. You see, John—John goes to Germany for a year, next July. So we thought—next June or July, Mother, just a little wedding like Ju's. You see, that's better than interrupting the term, or trying to settle down, when we'd have to move in July. And, Mother, I'm going to write Mrs. Carr-Boldt—she can get anyone to take my place. I want this year at home. I want to see more of Bruce and Ju, and sort of stand by darling little Beck! But it's for you, most of all, Mother," Margaret said with difficulty. "I've always loved you, Mother, but I haven't truly understood or appreciated you as I should. You don't know how wonderful I think you are—"

She broke off pitifully, "Oh, Mother!"

For her mother's arms had tightened about her, and the face against her own was wet.

"Are you talking?" said Rebecca, rearing herself up suddenly, with a web of bright hair falling over her shoulder. "You said your prayers with Mark last night," she said, reproachfully; "come over and say them with me tonight, Mother."

THE END